FRACTURE

ELYSE HOFFMAN

ISBN 978-1-952742-12-5 (eBook)
ISBN 978-1-952742-13-2 (Paperback)
ISBN 978-1-952742-17-0 (Hardcover)
ISBN 978-1-952742-16-3 (Large Print)

PROJECT613

Project 613 Publishing
https://www.elysehoffman.com/

To my grandfather David,
my grandmother Shirley,
my mother Lydia,
my father Richard,
and to God, Who makes all stories.

CHAPTER ONE

"You're going to have to go through me."

Eight-year-old Franz Keidel felt like his heart was about to stop. Today should have been a decent day—few days were *good* for him, but today was supposed to be *decent.*

He had found his father passed out on the old olive-green couch in their barren farmhouse. It was always a blessing whenever Herr Keidel drank himself into unconsciousness. It gave Franz freedom for a short time. Reprieve from the beatings and the screaming, from the man who seemed determined to punish Franz for a sin the boy couldn't remember committing.

Herr Keidel had been asleep, and so Franz had journeyed to see his neighbor. "Neighbor" perhaps wasn't the best term for Amos Auman since Franz's family farm was a decent three miles away from the Auman estate, but nonetheless it was worth the long walk to see his one and only friend.

Amos was his age, and he couldn't remember a time when they hadn't been close. Franz wasn't a very happy boy, but going to Amos' house and playing tennis or soccer gave him enough joy in his life. Enough that he hadn't leapt from the roof of his house.

Yet.

He'd certainly thought of jumping, but Amos had unwittingly stopped him. Amos had a weak gut and a big heart. Franz didn't like the idea that his friend would come looking for him and find a big puddle of blood and gore. He didn't like the idea of Amos gloomily staring at the tennis racket he usually reserved for Franz. He didn't like the idea of making the boy who made him smile cry.

So, he lived for the decent days. But when the decent days were interrupted, his resolve broke, and he began to seriously reconsider his decision to abstain from suicide.

Herr Keidel had ruined the decent day by waking up and stumbling onto the Aumans' property, swaying and staggering but still managing a regrettable amount of control over himself.

Franz was a small boy, smaller than most boys his age. Only Amos was smaller than he was. Franz's father, however, was a giant of a man. He had let himself go over the years: Franz had seen pictures of him in his youth, when he had been a soldier during the Great War, when he had been muscular and handsome. Now he had a round belly and sagging arms. But he was still a big man, big enough to hurt a little boy.

Franz's father approached with a birch stick in hand and a murderous flare in his murky eyes.

"You little *shit*," he snarled, smacking his palm with the makeshift rod. "You didn't do any of your chores! You fuck around...lazy little demon!"

Franz dropped the racket, knowing that trying to defend himself with such a weak weapon would only make things worse. He didn't bother asking for mercy or forgiveness, he didn't beg his father not to hurt him. He had learned long ago that such pleas would be pointless at best and a provocation at worst.

He didn't bother to pray that this beating wouldn't be harsh. He had learned long ago that if there was a God, He didn't care about weak little Franz Keidel.

He shielded his face with his arms, readying himself for the inevitable blows.

"You'll have to go through me."

But instead, there was a shuffling of feet and a defiant proclamation from a small voice. Franz looked up and was both touched and horrified to see that Amos had planted himself in front of his friend, arms outstretched, stubbornly rigid, like he was a mighty wall defending a castle keep.

Amos was not a mighty wall. He was a short skeleton of a boy with messy onyx hair and turquoise eyes. He was brave, certainly, and had a will of iron, but he wasn't strong. A gust of wind could knock him down, much less a blow from Herr Keidel.

"Amos, don't…" Franz begged, his voice breaking. He was used to being beaten, but the thought of watching Amos get hurt *for him, because of him*—Franz would rather take twelve beatings.

But despite Franz's plea, Amos didn't move. He dug his heels into the ground and glowered up at Herr Keidel, his cherubic face exuding furious defiance, his turquoise eyes blazing. Herr Keidel took a sloppy step backwards, as though the little boy's intensity surprised and frightened even him. Franz felt hope rise up in his chest.

But then Herr Keidel scowled, snarled, and lifted up the birch. Franz remembered a lesson he had learned long ago: *never hope it'll get better.*

Herr Keidel actually gave Amos a moment to move, to abandon this foolish bravery. But Amos didn't budge, and so when Franz's father swung his birch branch, he knocked Amos to the ground. A tooth flew from Amos' split lips and landed on the blood-splattered grass, and the branch—which must have been relatively weak, a poor choice for a beating stick, really—broke in two.

"Amos!" Franz screamed, rushing to his friend's side. "Amos, are you okay?! Amos!"

Amos let out a small whimper, which was good because that meant he hadn't been killed. Franz was so focused on his injured friend that he barely noticed or cared about his father. Herr Keidel mumbled something completely incoherent and dropped the broken branch, hastily shuffling back towards his farmstead. No doubt he remembered that Amos' father was a veteran of the Great War as well, and unlike Herr Keidel, Herr Auman hadn't let himself go.

And unlike Herr Keidel, Herr Auman loved his son.

And if he discovered what Herr Keidel had done, well…Franz would probably be an orphan by the time Herr Auman was through with his father. Which would have been nice. But Franz also didn't want to see Amos' father get tossed in jail for justified homicide, so he kept his mouth shut and didn't scream for Amos' parents, letting his father clumsily retreat.

"Oh, no, oh, no…are you okay? Can you talk…?" Franz whimpered, helping his friend sit up. Amos spat out a bloody wad of spittle. Franz whimpered.

"This is my fault...oh no...don't die, please…" Franz hiccupped. The nearest hospital was almost an hour away, and the Aumans didn't own a car. If Amos was really hurt...*if he dies because of me…*

The thought was too terrible to dwell on. If Amos died, then Franz would have nothing good in his life. If Amos died *protecting Franz*, then...well, that would simply be unbearable. The guilt would never leave his heart. The roof would be his only option.

"Nah gunna dah," Amos shook his head, pressed his palm against his bruised cheek, and somehow, *somehow*, he managed to smile at Franz. Amos's smile was always something of a marvel: bright and full and genuine. Franz was jealous of his smile most of the time. He wished he could smile like Amos.

Even now, showing off a gaping smile, a bloody smile, Amos still looked like himself. His far-too-good self. Franz felt a strange mixture of jealousy and adoration erupt in his chest, and although he had never been one for embraces, he grabbed his friend by the shoulders and tugged him into a tight hug.

"Never do that again, okay?" Franz begged. "I can take it. You can't...you don't have to do that for me, okay? I don't want you to get hurt. Promise me you'll never do that again, okay?"

And Amos simply sunk into the embrace, silently patting Franz's back and refusing to make a promise they both knew he wouldn't keep.

CHAPTER TWO

Many years later

"Private Keidel...Private Keidel, wake up!"
Franz Keidel almost jumped out of his SS uniform. His commanding officer, *Untersturmführer* Edmund Rahm, was standing above him with an absolutely murderous gleam in his green eyes. Almost by habit, as though signaling his loyalty would somehow assuage the *Untersturmführer's* fury, Private Keidel shoved his hand into the air.

"H-Heil Hitler..." Franz mumbled, and Edmund Rahm crossed his arms and tightened his jaw.

"The Führer's soldiers can't be napping on the job," Edmund declared curtly.

"Yes, sir," sighed Franz. He hadn't technically been napping *on the job*. He had been napping *on the way* to the job. He and the rest of his comrades had been sitting in the back of a covered van, twiddling their black-gloved thumbs and waiting to arrive at the house they had been called to.

Franz was fortunate that while Edmund Rahm always

held his men's shortcomings against them, he also wasn't one to drag things out. A few cold words and a declaration that Franz would have to work overtime to make up for his egregious negligence were enough for him. Franz grumbled his concession and scrambled out of the truck, hoping that the reports had been correct and their target was a member of the resistance. He really needed an excuse to beat someone up.

Or kill someone. Maybe a Jew or two. That would improve his mood. Make him feel less small. Less weak. Less like a little boy cowering before a giant and more like the perfect SS man he sought to be.

He glanced around the area and grunted when he realized they weren't at a house but a farm. Farms always summoned memories. Unpleasant memories of his father or pleasant memories of Amos, neither of which he wanted to dwell on. His father was dead and gone, but thinking about him evoked all the old feelings of fear and helplessness, and Franz despised being reminded of being so small, especially when he had just been chastised.

And Amos…he grunted. He'd been dreaming of his old friend more often, and the dreams were never pleasant. He kept dreaming of all the times Amos had suffered to try and lift him up, and it would grate at his soul and make him feel *small.*

He hadn't seen his friend in nearly a decade, not since the day the Führer had become Chancellor and Franz, seeing an escape, seeing hope in Hitler's promises that every German was strong and good, had fled from his family farm and pledged himself into the dictator's service.

He had left Amos behind that day, not wanting to steal him from his happy life and loving family. It had hurt to run without saying goodbye, but it had been for the best. He had only ever *taken* from Amos. Money, clothes, candy, love. Take, take, take. He hadn't wanted to see Amos again until he could finally *give* him something.

He sighed and plodded after his two comrades, Mueller and Dietrich, as they stiffly followed Edmund to the front porch of the small farmhouse. Franz glanced down at his SS uniform. Still a Private after all these years of service. He was loyal, of course, but his talents were physical. He could yank a Jew out of a basement and beat the living hell out of them, but that was the extent of his skill.

He refused to even attempt to track down his old friend until he could stand before him as an SS Sergeant. He had come far, but not far enough. He refused to lay eyes on Amos again until he was in a position where he could finally repay him for twelve years of friendship.

Don't think about him right now, Franz commanded himself. Thoughts of Amos were both too pleasant and too painful to dwell on during an operation. This work required focus and coldness. Love and regret and everything else that came with remembering Amos…it would just cloud his head, infect his vision when he looked upon the frightened faces of fugitive Jews. He forced his heart to harden and cleansed his thoughts of everything except the Cause. The Führer, a better Germany, a purer world.

Edmund crisply rapped on the door. Mueller snickered at the gaudy "Welcome" mat and wiped his mud-coated jackboots on it just as the door opened. Mueller had bragged several times that he had been a skilled jeweler before joining the SS, but Franz had difficulty imagining the crass SS man carefully setting a diamond in a necklace. He could see Mueller being a jewel-thief, certainly, but a jeweler? He had his doubts.

An old man wearing a cross necklace opened the door. They had been told that the owner of this home was a member of the Black Foxes, a resistance group that operated as an underground railroad for fleeing Jews. Black Foxes weren't all fighters, and it wasn't at all strange for some members of their ranks to be seemingly feeble and helpless.

Franz stared at the man's aged face, which was partially concealed behind a bush of greying facial hair. Still, he saw some telltale signs that their tip had been a good one: tightened lips, rapid blinking, and when the old man raised up his hand and greeted the SS men with "Heil Hitler," he did so with the sort of tone that indicated he was biting back a stutter.

Edmund Rahm greeted him with all the graciousness of a weasel with a hernia. "Gilbert Winkler. We're here to search your home."

"I...what?!" sputtered Old Man Winkler, and Franz had to bite back a chuckle. As much as he was a pain to work for, Edmund Rahm was quite good at catching suspects off-guard with his directness. Most Germans at least expected the *pretense* of civility from the educated intellectuals of the SS. Edmund Rahm was never one for false smiles and forced pleasantries.

Actually, he wasn't really one for smiles and pleasantries at all, even of the non-forced variety.

Actually, Franz had no idea what a smiling Edmund Rahm would look like. Probably terrifying. Terrifying and unnatural. It would be like seeing a snake smile.

Without even waiting for an answer, Edmund Rahm strolled inside, pushing past the old man. Mueller followed with a snide sneer. Dietrich gave Winkler a quiet greeting in an almost apologetic tone, as though he was a babysitter shepherding an unruly gaggle of toddlers through a toy store. Franz didn't even look at the old man as he walked in, instead glancing about the house.

It was absurdly tiny: a small sitting room attached to a little kitchen with a table set for one, a simple little bedroom, one bathroom. The furnishings were minimal as well: one cozy chair, a table that almost looked like a dresser sitting against a wall, a state-sponsored radio that Joseph Goebbels' Propaganda Ministry made sure was in the home of every German, and one single bookshelf laden with Christian books.

"Where is your copy of *Mein Kampf?*" Edmund Rahm asked.

"It's here!" snapped the old man, throwing open a drawer and yanking out a copy of Hitler's autobiography, which was stiff and covered in dust, indicating that the old man owned it out of necessity and not affection for the dictator. "Would you also like to see my Iron Cross? I earned it fighting in the Great War! Fighting for this nation!"

"Truly," Edmund grumbled, glancing at a Bible sitting by the large cozy chair, which was worn down, dog-marked, and clearly well-loved. Edmund's emerald eyes shifted from the Bible to the neglected Mein Kampf, and a sneer that approached a smile almost too much for Franz's comfort grew on his face. "A German hero like you surely has nothing to hide."

The SS *Untersturmführer* strolled over to the radio, casually flicking it on. His brow knit in disappointment when he was greeted with Goebbels' nasally screech. The Führer's herald was yelling about Jews again. Edmund Rahm had obviously been hoping that the supposed Black Fox would be listening to Black Fox Radio, but Winkler hadn't been so careless.

"I have nothing to hide," Winkler insisted, curling one gnarled hand around the cross pendant.

"Then you won't mind if we have a look around your property," Edmund said, waving for his men to tear the place apart. Mueller and Dietrich searched the bedroom while Franz stayed in the sitting area, shoving the bookshelf out of the way, searching for a hidden trapdoor or a cellar where the Black Fox could be hiding Jews.

As he searched, he felt like someone was watching him. Winkler's anxious eyes followed him as he tore up the carpets, but he could feel a more powerful force observing his every move.

Franz looked up and felt a shiver claw its way up his spine when he realized there was a painting hanging on the wall, a painting of Jesus Christ. Somehow, even though the picture was still, the eyes were drawn in a strange way, the pupils almost too wide, too all-seeing. It felt like no matter where he went, the eyes were watching.

He grunted. Unsettling, certainly, but only insofar as a painting of a monster would be. He didn't believe in monsters, no matter how many times the Jews he pulled from basements called him one. He believed in enemies, in science. He believed that races were biologically different and pitted against one another by the brutal laws of nature. But God? No. Not Jesus or God or anything of the sort. He didn't believe in any of it.

Because he remembered being small and weak and begging whatever God had created him to help him, to give him strength, to make the beatings stop, and receiving nothing but silence in response. He would rather believe in nothing than believe that there was a God who simply didn't give a damn about him.

He grunted and touched the swastika armband, trying to draw strength from the symbol, from his own cross. He didn't believe in Gods or magic or anything like that, but he believed in Hitler. Jesus Christ had never answered his pleas for help, but Hitler had. Hitler had given him a home, a place where he was worth something. Hitler had taken a weak little boy and made him strong. He still remembered being fourteen years old and getting an opportunity to shake the Führer's hand during a parade. It had been the greatest moment of his life, like grasping the hand of an angel.

He remembered that moment as he ripped Winkler's house to shreds, as he coldly ignored the whimpers and pleas from the old man. He remembered grasping Hitler's hand, and a zealous desire to hunt down his messiah's enemies filled him.

Search as he might, however, he found nothing. No cellar, not even a loose floorboard. Dietrich and Mueller soon returned, equally empty-handed.

"I told you I had nothing to hide," Winkler said, tightening his grip on the cross and glancing at his picture of Christ in a reverently grateful manner. Edmund scoffed, marched towards the small dinner table, and gestured to the chair.

"Sit, Herr Winkler," the *Untersturmführer* commanded, and after a second of hesitation, Winkler obeyed, shuffling hastily past a smirking Mueller and plopping down in his chair. Edmund stood on the other side of the table, leaning over the stained wood surface. Goebbels chastised the traitors in their midst.

"Turn that off," Edmund commanded, and Dietrich turned the knob, silencing the propagandist even as his howls still rang in Franz's ears, giving him the strength of a crusader.

"You'll answer some questions," Edmund said before glancing at his men. "Mueller, you stay with me. Dietrich, Keidel, you go outside and search the barns."

"W-wait, you can't do that!" cried Winkler, starting to stand. "You'll disturb the animals, you'll…!"

One cold scowl from Edmund silenced the old man, who sunk back down in his chair, his lip wobbling as he stared at Jesus' all-seeing visage. Franz smirked. The barns, then. It had to be the barns.

He and Dietrich strolled outside and leapt over the

fence, marching towards the back of the property. Winkler's farm was relatively meager: a henhouse and two barns, one of which was closer to the house and emanated bleats and the smell of shit. The other barn stood on a hill in the distance, small and silent.

"Aww, hey there, kitty!" Dietrich crooned, and Franz felt something small and lithe brush against his leg. He looked down and barely kept a smile off his face when he saw a small feline rubbing against his jackboots, oblivious to how much these guests were troubling his master.

Franz stooped down and ran his hand along the cat's ruddy fur. A barn cat. A brown tabby. He bit the inside of his cheek. It looked far too much like Amos' old cat, Mausefalle. The thought of that mean old feline almost made him chuckle. Mausefalle had been the Auman family's resident barn cat who had kept their feed free of rats and mice. He had been good at his job, and Amos had loved him like he was a house pet.

Amos had loved Mausefalle, but the feeling hadn't been mutual. For some reason, all animals had always despised Amos, and Mausefalle in particular had hated the sweet little boy. Franz almost smiled as he remembered how Amos would coo and pull Mausefalle into the hug, only for the cat to yowl and flail and scratch at the boy's soft skin. Amos had never despised the cat for its behavior, though. He had loved it, regardless.

Meanwhile, Franz, who had never been particularly *fond* of animals but didn't *dislike* them either, seemed to be a magnet for nature. Mausefalle had hated Amos but loved Franz, purring whenever the Keidel boy had visited the Auman Farm and resting in his lap whenever little Franz felt miserable.

Franz had always felt bad about that, about stealing Amos' cat from him, and he had felt worse when his friend refused to be jealous. Amos would always sit at a distance, watch Mausefalle snuggle into his friend's lap, and smile.

Franz shook his head and stood up, shooing the cat to Dietrich, who apparently had less compunctions about coddling a potential Black Fox's pet. The younger SS man started scratching behind the feline's ears.

"Hm," muttered Franz. "Animals are in there..." He looked towards the bigger barn. "So that one on the hill must be an isolation barn."

"A wha...?" Dietrich mumbled, not looking up from the cat, smiling like an absolute idiot when the feline ran its rough tongue over his black-gloved hand.

"Barn for ill animals, so they won't get the others sick," sighed Franz, pinching his brow. Why couldn't Edmund have sent Mueller outside with him?

Well, Franz thought, looking up at the distant isolation barn, *if this man is a Black Fox, it's more likely that whatever Jews he's hiding are in that barn. And Dietrich...*

He glanced down at his fellow SS man, who was trying to coax the barn cat into accepting a belly rub.

It's...probably better if I'm the one to actually find the Jews. Dietrich will get himself killed on his own. That or he'll try to pet the Jews.

"You go search that one," Franz commanded, pointing towards the larger structure. "I'll check the isolation barn."

"Okay!" Dietrich agreed, scooping the cat under one arm and marching towards the larger barn. Franz raised an eyebrow and wondered why Dietrich felt the need to take the cat with him.

Maybe he's stealing it, Franz mused as he set off up the hill towards the isolation barn. *All well and good. It'll need a new home when we shoot its owner. Maybe he's planning on throwing it at any Black Foxes he comes across...*

That thought made him smirk. Something was

comical about the image: Dietrich, criminally new to the SS and criminally unprepared for a real battle, shrieking like a little girl and tossing his new kitten at a murderous Black Fox.

It was funny, but it was also an issue. Dietrich was as pure a German as they came, but he was still too soft. If they found a Jew at this house, it would be his first.

Maybe I should let him kill it, Franz thought. *He needs to get some grime under his fingernails. He's got to toughen up. He's too much like Amos right now.*

Franz grunted at the thought. Amos had been a wonderful friend, but he wouldn't have lasted five seconds in the SS. A boy who loved a cat that nearly scratched his eyes out wouldn't have even made it through training camp. Franz still wasn't sure how Dietrich *had* made it through training unless there was a toughness to him that simply wasn't visible.

That was possible. He had met SS men who were gentle as lambs most of the time but became cold and merciless as a lion when confronted with even the smallest Jewish child.

It occurred to Franz as he opened the barn door and slipped inside that the old man was probably hiding a child. Maybe a few children. Most older Black Foxes handled the little ones, shepherding them about until they could procure false papers or sneak them over enemy lines. He grunted. He had killed many Jews before, women and men. He had hit children before, and he had sent them to camps, but he hadn't shot one. Not yet.

Maybe I won't save this one for Dietrich after all…if it's a child, I'll do it myself.

He encased his heart in a cocoon of ice and pulled out his gun. The barn was barren save for a few piles of hay and a square bale of straw that sat against a wall, almost like a makeshift chair or couch. There was an unlit lantern sitting in a far corner, instantly putting Franz on edge. An oil lamp in a barn full of flammable hay? In a barn supposedly only meant for ill animals who wouldn't care one bit about having a light...

His gaze shifted to one particularly large pile of hay covered in a massive blanket. A blanket fit for a horse, yes. But Winkler didn't have any horses.

No. A blanket fit for a hiding Jew to curl up in when the frosty nights became nearly unbearable. He peered closely at the large pile and smirked when he saw little bits of hay trembling.

*Got you...*he thought with the satisfaction of a cat that had cornered a rat, aiming his gun at the Jew's hiding spot.

"Come out. Hands up. Now. Or I start shooting," Franz declared, his tone rigid. No Jew would test him when he sounded so soulless.

There was a mere second of hesitation. He pulled back the hammer of his gun. The *click* echoed through the barn.

"W-wait!" A small voice came from the hay and two hands popped out. Franz almost smirked at the silliness of the sight.

"All of you, out," the SS man commanded.

"T-there's only me..." the hiding Jew insisted, and Franz knew better than to believe him. The voice was that of an adult man, albeit a young one. It wasn't unusual for the men to surrender first in an attempt to keep children or wives hidden.

"Out! Now!" the Nazi snapped, and the hay shifted about as the Jew revealed himself.

A young man crawled out of the hay, dressed in dark, ragged clothing that was two sizes too big for him. A yellow star was stitched onto his chest, right above his heart. He was a small man, small and skinny, which wasn't surprising since Herr Winkler probably couldn't spare much of his farm's bounty, not without alerting the authorities.

The Jew stood up, raising his hands above his head and trembling like a newborn lamb. His hair was dark and somewhat curly, with little strands of hay clinging to his locks. He looked up at Franz, tears leaking from his eyes.

Turquoise eyes.

The cocoon of ice fractured. *No. No. It can't be.*

Franz narrowed his eyes at the man, scrutinizing his every feature. This quaking creature didn't hold himself with the joviality of his old friend, but…

"Your name," Franz commanded.

"W-what…?" the Jew stuttered, and when he opened his mouth, Franz saw that he was missing a tooth.

"Your name!" Not a shout, a hiss, practically a plea for the Jew to say any name except…

"A-Amos Auman, please…"

The Jew—no, *Amos*—regarded the SS man with terror for one more moment, a small sob wracking his body as he tried to plead for mercy.

But then he must have seen the SS man's monstrous mask break as horror bloomed on Franz's face.

"F-Franz…?" Amos' uncertain whisper was at once pained and hopeful.

To Franz, there was silence in the barn save for Amos's heavy breathing and the pounding of his own pulse in his ears. He felt like his soul was being ripped in two and sewn back together over and over again. It felt like he was being shot, but not given the reprieve of eternal slumber.

They didn't say a word to one another, but unspoken questions hung between the Jew and the SS man. *What are you doing here? How are you one of them? This doesn't make sense.*

It didn't make sense. Jews were soulless parasites, a

race of devils that Hitler's black-clothed angels were obliged to decimate.

But Amos…Amos who had loved a cat that hated him, Amos who had defended Franz when he was weak, Amos who had celebrated Christmas with him and stolen sweets for him…

Was it all a trick? That thought made the shield of ice start to reform. *A trick. All a trick…*

Except…Amos gaped at him, still missing that tooth from when he had stretched out his arms and protected a boy that even God wouldn't defend.

No. It hadn't been a trick. He could see it in Amos' eyes: affection buried by uncertainty, by a fear that Franz would…

Would…

The gun felt heavy in Franz's hand, and he realized he was aiming right at the yellow star on Amos' chest.

It felt like time froze right then. His head buzzed with Hitler's speeches, with Goebbels' sermons on the corrupting power of Jewry, with Himmler's insistence that all Jews had to be exterminated. From the baby in the cradle to the childhood best friend.

But…

But this was *Amos.* Amos, who he had known since he was a baby, Amos who had been his only reason for staying off the farmhouse roof for years, Amos who he had always wanted to repay for his years of kindness.

And now he could. It would just cost him his soul. The soul he had sworn to the SS, to Hitler. If he spared Amos, what then? Could he still call himself an SS man? He felt his hand burn. He would be unworthy of his Führer. A hypocrite of the first order, like a priest who preached abstinence while having three mistresses.

It would be wrong. Morally wrong. It would go against

everything he had done, everything he had worked for. Everything he had killed for.

But…

Amos was watching him like he was a childhood pet that had run away and gone feral, like he wasn't sure whether to approach with love or caution.

If he turned Amos in, Franz knew he would never be able to close his eyes again. Not without seeing the hope in those turquoise eyes die.

If he shot him…it would be merciful, really. Better than what he would get in a camp.

That thought made him want to jump off a farmhouse roof.

The feeling like he was being torn in two over and over got worse. Rip went his soul, and then a burning fire soldered it back together. Rip, burn, rip, burn.

He hadn't cried since he was a child, but he wanted to cry right then.

"Keidel!" Dietrich's voice startled him from his ponderings. Amos' eyes blazed with fear, with a plea.

Rip, burn, rip, burn.

"Keidel, did you find anything?"

You have to make a choice.

"Keidel?" The voice was getting closer.

"Franz…" Amos had never sounded so afraid when they were kids. Not even when he had stood before a snarling giant.

You'll have to go through me.

Franz lowered his gun and betrayed his nation with one word. "No!" he shouted.

He nudged his head towards the pile of hay. Amos only hesitated for a second, rewarding Franz's treachery with a smile so radiant that the ice around the SS man's heart melted away. The Jew dove back into his hiding place.

Franz took in a deep gulp of air and fixed a nonplussed expression onto his face. He shoved his gun back into its holster and exited the barn, nearly bumping into Dietrich.

"There's nobody here," Franz declared, his voice calm despite the battle that was raging in his soul as he spoke. "Let's go."

Dietrich believed him.

Edmund Rahm believed him.

Winkler gave him a strange look, like he was a demon that had saved a baby from a burning building.

They left the farm empty-handed except for Winkler's cat, which Dietrich insisted on commandeering despite Edmund's grumbles of protest.

"Well, that was a waste of time," Mueller grunted as they piled back into the Jew-free truck, watching with a smirk as Dietrich crooned over his new pet.

"We should make him a mascot," Dietrich suggested, scratching the cat's ears. "Poor thing, look how tiny he is! And he's so sweet!"

"You're such a child, Dietrich," Mueller chuckled. "Mascot!"

"He needs a good name!" Dietrich declared. "Keidel, what do you think? Keidel...?"

Franz was staring out the open back flap of the van, his gaze lingering on the isolation barn as it vanished into the distance.

"Keidel, are you okay?"

"Mausefalle."

"What?"

"Name it Mausefalle," Franz declared. Dietrich glanced from his comrade to his stolen cat and smiled.

"Mausefalle, that's a good one!" Dietrich laughed.

Franz took in a shuddering breath, trying desperately to calm himself. The sensation of his soul tearing itself apart continued on as Hitler's voice echoed in his ear, chastising him for his actions. *Traitor. Traitor. Traitor.*

But Amos's voice silenced his internal Führer. He remembered watching Mausefalle claw at his friend's chest, leaving vast wounds. He remembered watching Amos forgive the cat. He remembered sighing and rolling his eyes and saying, *Amos, why do you even like that cat? He's a little monster.*

And Amos had given him a smile that could melt an iceberg, the same smile he had offered in the barn. He'd smiled and shown off the gap in his grin and declared, *He's my monster!*

Perhaps he had done the wrong thing, but if doing the right thing meant killing Amos, Franz would rather be a villain.

CHAPTER THREE

For the second time in two days, Herr Gilbert Winkler heard a terse knocking on his door.

For the second time in two days, Gilbert Winkler opened his front door and found himself facing a scowling SS man.

For the second time in two days, the man who was hiding a Jew in his barn forced a smile onto his face and raised up his hand, greeting the Knight of the Black Order with a sugary, "Heil Hitler."

But the SS man didn't lift up his hand and return the show of loyalty. He crossed his arms, tapped his jackboots on the muddy 'Welcome' mat, and said, "Don't play games. I know you're hiding Amos."

Gilbert very nearly fell down and died of a heart attack right then, but fortunately, the SS man must have seen his distress. The furious mask faltered, and the Nazi held up his hands as though prepared to catch the old man if he collapsed.

"I'm not here to arrest anyone!" he cried. "Amos is…"

"You're the man from a few days ago. Amos' old friend." Gilbert exhaled, his terrified expression morphing into a genuine smile. "Amos told me what you did. God bless you, young man. You did a good thing."

A good thing. The thought both amused and exasperated Franz Keidel. Betraying his nation, his principles, his Führer, his messiah...a good thing. He curled his black-gloved hands into tight fists and grunted, "I'd like to speak to him."

He felt the Jesus picture's gaze upon him and suddenly felt very much like running away and forgetting this whole thing, but before he could even consider it, Gilbert grabbed him by the arm. He wrenched his limb from the old man's grasp, barely keeping the instinctual discomfort from showing on his face.

"I know where he is. I just wanted to ask permission," Franz grunted. Gilbert curled his hand around the cross decorating his neck and smiled gently.

"Of course. Thank you. If you need anything, let me know."

Franz skittered away from the front door with more eagerness that was probably becoming of an SS man, but he wasn't here as an SS man. He was here as Franz Keidel. As Amos Auman's best friend. And it felt like he was becoming a stranger because he hadn't been *that* Franz Keidel in almost a decade.

He slowed his march as he drew nearer and nearer to Amos' barn. Gilbert had let the chickens out to pasture, and practically on cue, the little birds started trailing after the SS man. Franz felt his face turn scarlet.

Not again. He remembered when he was little and he would blunder onto the Auman Farm when Amos' mother had let out the chickens. For some reason, even though he never fed them or even pretended to be fond of them, the dumb birds had followed little Franz all over the farmstead, clucking at his heels and gazing up at him like he was some sort of avian messiah. And

Amos would watch the stupid display and laugh and call him…

"Hahnchen." Little Rooster.

Franz entered the barn, slammed the door shut just before the gaggle of hens could follow him inside, and turned to see a smirking Amos leaning against the splintery wall. The fugitive's turquoise eyes shimmered with boyish mischief as he dropped Franz's old pet name, and whereas two days ago his expression had shifted from fearful uncertainty to surprised relief, he now regarded his old friend with a smile.

Amos' smile was strange. It was nice, just like it always had been when he was young, but it faltered slightly at the edges. Like it had been broken and just barely put back together for Franz's sake.

"Good to see some things haven't changed," Amos said, his tone taking on a slightly sour tune as his eyes roamed Franz' uniformed body. Franz felt his cheeks flush, and he crossed his arms over his Nazi medals, affixing his old friend with a glare that he realized from the way Amos winced must have been almost exactly like the look Frau Auman had given them on the multitude of occasions where they had messed up.

"You're a Jew," Franz said. It wasn't a question: half an accusation, half a plea.

"I am?" It was a tribute to Franz's training that he was able to repress a smile of amusement as Amos feigned shock, looking down at the yellow Star-of-David sewn onto his breast.

"Well, would you look at that!?" he gasped, and Franz had to bite the inside of his cheek. Damn Amos, always able to make him smile after all these years.

"You never told me you were a Jew," Franz said. "I knew you all my life, and you never told me."

"Not *all* your life," Amos pointed out, and Franz felt

like he'd been stung by a bee. His friend had never spoken to him in such a bitter, almost angry tone. It didn't suit Amos' pleasant voice.

"Anyway, I never thought it mattered," Amos sighed. "As far as I always knew, I was never more a Jew than you were a Christian. I was born a Jew, sure, but we never did the ceremonies. It wasn't important until Hitler made it important."

He let out a dour chuckle and sat on the bale of hay that seemingly acted as a couch. "So…sorry, Hahnchen. Didn't mean to keep secrets."

"I…I…" Franz almost kicked himself. He had already betrayed the Reich, but he was still an SS officer, and stuttering like he was still eight years old wasn't becoming of Hitler's elite.

It felt like he should have been angry. He should have been furious that Amos had lied to him all his life. Pretended to be German, pretended to be good, pretended to have a soul…

But…no, it couldn't have been pretend.

Jews couldn't feel, Jews didn't have a soul, but no soulless creature would have dressed a helpless seven-year-old's wounds and whispered that one day they would run away together. No soulless creature would get between a six-foot-two drunk and furious Herr Keidel when he was about to beat little Franz with a thick hunk of birch. *You'll have to go through me!*

No. No, Amos wasn't soulless.

So maybe he wasn't a Jew. Not really. Not fully. Half-Jew, half-human. Special. Maybe he was just a mutant among his race. One in a million. A Jew with a soul.

Franz suddenly became acutely aware that Amos was alone in the barn. Amos had a family. He had a good family. He wouldn't have run away from them. Not unless he had to.

25

"Where's…?" Franz started to say, glancing about the corners of the empty barn. "How did you get here, Amos?"

"Well, first I put one foot in front of the other…"

"Be serious, please," sighed Franz, inching a bit closer to his old friend when he realized that the chasm between them was just as literal as it was figurative. He made sure the barn door was locked and then, failing to find any place to sit with dignity, plopped down on the floor with his legs crisscrossed like he was a boy again. A boy waiting to hear a sad story.

"Oooh, serious!" Amos chuckled. "Well, that's a tall order. Y'know my old man served in the war…the war before the war we're fighting now. The Great War. Is that gonna make this the Greater War? The Greatest War? Doesn't feel that great…"

"The Great War Part Two?" Franz suggested despite himself, still refusing to smile but unable to keep an amused lilt from entering his voice. Amos cackled.

"I see you're just as creative as ever! The boy who used to name every goat 'Goaty' is still in there somewhere."

"I never said he left," Franz said. "Naming goats isn't one of my official SS duties."

"Nah…guess it wouldn't be. Anyway, what was I saying? Ah, my old man! He served with Herr Winkler, old wartime buddies. I know you and your SS pals thought Gilbert was a Black Fox, but no…no connection at all. I wish there was, but he doesn't even know how to get on Black Fox Radio on his own."

"So…he's an old friend of your father. Then where's your father?"

Amos' smile vanished and his face…Amos' gentle, boyish features didn't suit the look he gave his own mud-encrusted shoes. Haunted, hollow.

"He's dead," Amos said. "So's Mama. And Uta."

"Your parents and your sister," Franz murmured. He hadn't been well-acquainted with the Aumans aside from Amos. He knew Amos' father had been a war veteran, and he knew that he hadn't beaten his children, and that fact had made him at once relieved for and jealous of Amos. Frau Auman had sometimes looked at him with soft longing in her eyes, like she wanted to pick him up and hug him but knew better.

Amos' sister, Uta—oh, Uta, Uta, Uta! He had rarely actually encountered his friend's older sister, but he had gotten an earful *about* her. Whenever things had been too tense, whenever misery had descended upon him, Amos would clear it away with a story about his crazy bitch of a sister. Uta put dead spiders in her mother's shampoo, Uta kicked her last boyfriend so hard in the crotch that he lost a testicle, Uta stole Amos' birthday presents and sold them to buy a new flute. Uta this, Uta that, *you're lucky you don't have a sister, Franz!*

And Franz would never feel lucky, but he would appreciate Amos' little anecdotes, however exaggerated.

Amos had often cackled and declared that he wished Uta was dead. He had gotten his wish apparently, and it didn't feel real. It didn't feel *right*. It should have felt right because Uta and the Aumans were Jews, but it didn't, and the fact that it didn't made Franz once again feel like his chest was being torn apart.

"I'm...sorry, Amos," he stuttered, and saying that felt wrong too because they were Jews and they deserved it, but they didn't because they were Amos' family and he loved them.

"You are, aren't you?" Amos sighed. "What about you, Franz? What are you doing in the SS? You're a good person."

"I...I'm in the SS *because* I'm a good person, Amos," Franz said, and before he could even begin to elaborate further, Amos burst into a bout of laughter so loud that Franz was worried *Untersturmführer* Rahm would be able to hear him all the way back at SS HQ. It wasn't a good laugh. It wasn't the laugh he remembered Amos had once possessed.

"Oh! Oh, okay!" Amos finally cried when he managed to stop his cackling fit enough to let out a coherent phrase. "Oh, that's a good one, Franz! You never did have a decent sense of humor, but that's...that's *funny!*"

"It's not..." Franz started, and he knew without needing a mirror that his face must have been absolutely scarlet. "It's...I'm not joking, Amos."

"Well, Hahnchen, if that's true, then I'm guessing you think that what the SS does is *good*. The thing the SS does being hunting down and killing Jews. But be that the case, my friend, why didn't you turn me in?"

That feeling. It was back, and it was worse than before. At least when that very same question had been running through Franz's mind for the past two days, it had been *his*, private, he didn't actually have to answer. But Amos was looking at him, his turquoise eyes burrowing right through him. Franz felt like some sort of mischievous magical force had stripped him of his SS garb, like he was standing before Amos completely nude.

"You're...you're *you*," he stuttered, and though he wanted to say more, explain why Amos being Amos mattered, why Amos being Amos made it *different*, he found his tongue irreparably tied and couldn't say another word.

Nevertheless, Amos seemed to soften at his response. His smug smile became gentle, genuine, and Franz felt relief settle on his heart. *There we go, there's his old smile.*

"Well, I'm not one to look a gift horse in the mouth," Amos sighed. "Horses hate me, usually."

An out. Thank God. "Animals still hate you?"

chuckled Franz. "Being honest, I'm kind of surprised the old man is hiding you in a barn. I…y'know…if he'd put you in a barn with any animals, then they would'a killed you and saved the SS the trouble."

"Ha! I warned him! Initially, he tried to hide me in the regular barn, said the goats would bleat and keep me hidden and it would be easier…nope! First hour I was in there, six different goats attacked me, *six*! Thank God he had this barn for sick animals. Now I just have to pray none of his animals *actually* get sick."

"Between the animals and the…emptiness…" Franz glanced about the barn. "I'm surprised you haven't gone completely crazy. What do you even do all day?"

"When I'm not cowering in hay piles and hoping that the SS man who's about to uncover me is actually my old neighbor? Read, mostly."

"Read?! You?!" exclaimed Franz in disbelief as Amos crawled over to one particularly tall bunch of hay and uncovered a small stack of thoroughly water-damaged hardbacks. Amos had been the worst student in school; it was a miracle he even remembered how to read. He had often begged Franz to help him with his assignments because he simply couldn't focus on words written on paper. Franz had quite literally read entire books aloud to him. If Franz had read something aloud, it would stick somehow. Amos had once said he had a magic voice.

Franz touched his neck and found himself clearing his throat, pondering if his voice still carried the same "magic" after all these years.

"You don't know the half of it," Amos sighed. "I'm real desperate. Winkler tries to get me books that aren't pro-Nazi, but I'm pretty sure those have all been burned. It's all right, though. Winkler sometimes has me come in and we listen to the radio, we talk a little…we don't have much to talk about, but...oh well. Bein' bored's good. Ghettos and camps are exciting. Boring is safe. But!"

Amos suddenly slammed his hands on the ground. "Enough about me! What I do here ain't as important as what you're planning on doing here! Seems like you're not eager to have a debate about the merits of Hitler's political system, so why did you come back? Just to interrogate me?"

"Yes...well...no...I...erm...I haven't seen you in a while and I was..."

He searched for the right word for too long and Amos leaned forward, his insufferable smirk back in place. "Worried?" he guessed, and Franz huffed.

"Curious," the SS man said.

"Well...hope I sated your curiosity. You can go now, if you want."

Turquoise eyes glistened. Damn Amos couldn't read a book to save his life, but he could certainly read Franz even after all of these years.

But Franz wasn't a little boy anymore, and he had what he wanted. Answers, if vaguely given. Confirmation. He stood up.

"I can't stay long," he declared. "I have to get back to work."

Amos's smile twitched. "To the SS."

"Yeah."

"To killing Jews."

Franz's eyes narrowed. "If you don't want me to come back..."

"I didn't say I don't want you to come back," Amos said. "If you don't want to come back, then that's on you, but I don't not want you to come back. Makes sense?"

"Completely," snorted Franz, and he let his smile emerge from its long hibernation. "Then I potentially might not fail to return later. We definitely have more to talk about."

"Can I just assume that you aren't going to tell your bosses about me?" Amos said, fishing a book out from under the hay pile and plopping it in his lap.

Franz grunted. Of course he wouldn't, couldn't, and Amos knew it now. If he had any intention of turning him in, he would have done so before.

"You know I won't," Franz said, almost spitting it like an accusation, and Amos shrugged.

"I'd like to believe that I still know you...despite everything," the fugitive sighed, and the ripping feeling in Franz's chest became too intense, too awful. With a grunt, Franz bade farewell to his old friend and wished him good luck.

He should have stayed away after that. Been sated with his answers. Been content to leave Amos alone.

Alone in that barn. *Alone.*

Amos would have never left Franz alone in such an awful place. Alone and hungry. Alone and bored.

Franz had barely returned to the office, and he was already plotting out his next visit.

CHAPTER FOUR

H err Keidel had often withheld food when Franz's existence became particularly onerous to him. Amos had always given Franz what he could spare. Franz probably owed Amos at least a foot of his six-foot stature. He would have been malnourished if not for him.

Amos' family had never had much themselves. Franz had always assumed with not a small amount of guilt that Amos' shortness was partially his fault. Amos had quite literally given Franz food off his own plate, and his health had suffered.

So really, feeding Amos wasn't a crime against the state. It *was*, but it wasn't because it was just returning a favor. And it was perfectly honorable and perfectly German to return a favor.

His knees started to feel weak after two weeks of giving the starving Jew half his own rations. Major Sigmund Rahm, Edmund's older brother and the troop's leader, heard Franz's stomach growl and quipped that he would have to increase Private Keidel's rations or else the Jews would quite literally hear the SS man coming.

"Sorry, Chief, I'm…I guess I'm having a growth spurt," Franz replied, trying to shield the nervousness in his voice and thankfully managing to fool Sigmund.

"You'd better not, or you'll make the rest of the men feel inadequate! Times are good now, Keidel, you just had to ask."

And so he got more food, and so did Amos. Times were good indeed.

Amos certainly seemed to think his lot had improved. Franz visited as often as he could. He would bring food, water, coffee, and sometimes even delicacies.

"Chocolate!" Amos all but squealed when Franz pulled a small candy bar out of his pocket, slightly melted from his journey to the farm but still more than edible. It was completely impossible to maintain a neutral expression when Amos snatched up the bar and glowed.

"God Almighty, I haven't had a chocolate bar in…two years?" Amos muttered. "In the Ghetto, it was worth a lot. Whenever we snagged one, we'd have to sell it right away for something more…calorical? What's the word?"

"Filling?" Franz suggested, stiffening a bit. When they talked, they usually kept their conversational topics tightly constrained to memories from when they were boys. He didn't talk about being in the SS, and Amos didn't talk about being a Jew. It was easier for both of them that way. It made Franz almost forget what he was doing.

"Nope, that's not the right word," Amos said. "Hey, remember when we were eight and we stole that candy bar from Herr Schwartz's candy shop?"

"*We*?! It was *your* idea!"

"Sticky fingers!" Amos waved his hand and giggled. "Anyway, he deserved it. Almost a whole mark for a candy bar?! Highway robbery! Remember he grabbed me and threatened to cut my hand off, but you snatched his broom and just *nailed* him in the balls…and his *scream*…"

"And then Frau Henriksen came in screaming because she thought her *daughter* made that noise. And he didn't even tell our parents because he was so embarrassed." Franz felt nostalgic mirth bubbling up in his chest and he couldn't help but smile wider. Every visit to Amos' barn made his training break more and more as he remembered what it was like to be around someone who knew him.

Amos cackled. "And then we split it fifty-fifty even though I tried to give you a bigger half 'cause you saved the day. Good times!"

"Good times," Franz concurred. He never would have described his childhood as being "good," but the time he had spent with Amos had been more than good. Better than his SS training. Better than getting a handshake from the Führer? Probably not.

Amos was looking down at the chocolate bar with a thoughtful smile, his turquoise eyes taking on a softness that made them strangely magnetic. Franz almost winced when the J—when *Amos* broke the precious bar in two.

"Here, let's split it!" the fugitive suggested, and the SS man chuckled, glancing down at the bar (which, he noticed with not a small amount of amusement and exasperation, hadn't been broken evenly—Amos was offering him the bigger piece.)

"Why would we split it, Amos?" he half chuckled. "I'm…" *An SS man. A free man. A person.*

"I can get chocolate whenever I want."

"So you can bring more later! And we can split that too! Here, c'mon, for old time's sake."

"Amos…" Franz started to sigh, and he looked at Amos' face and…well, the fugitive's cheeks were scarlet and full now, no longer hollow. He wasn't starving anymore. He looked goo—he looked *healthy*. And it looked like he *really* wanted to share.

Plus, Franz was pretty hungry. He took the large chunk of chocolate and gave his old friend a conciliatory smile. Amos lifted up his smaller piece.

"Cheers?" he offered.

Franz could feel his inner SS man screaming, writhing in pain at the indignity, but he tapped his candy chunk against Amos' and concurred. "Cheers."

HE NOTICED after Amos stopped looking sickly that Amos actually looked pretty good. Well, pretty good for a man who lived in a barn. Clean-shaved and…well, *clean*.

"Old Man Gilbert lets me into the house at night to bathe and shave," Amos explained when Franz asked about this, rubbing his hand along his nicked chin. "Can't stand beards, don't know how other Jews deal with 'em."

Franz unwillingly visualized Amos with a long beard like a Rabbi, like an Orthodox Jew. It almost made him laugh, but it also made him feel a little sick.

"You wouldn't look good with a beard," Franz said, and Amos' eyes glistened.

"Does that imply that I do look good *without* a beard?" he queried in a teasing tone, and Franz didn't like that he had to change the subject lest the truth somehow tumble out of his lips.

"So, why did you join the SS?"

"We've discussed this."

"We really haven't."

"The Fatherland needs my service."

35

"The *Father*land."

"Amos…"

"What exactly do you owe the Fatherland?"

"My life, my blood, my everything. Can we not discuss this?"

"If you owe it everything and you really think all Jews are a threat…"

"You're different."

"I'm really not."

"Can we talk about something else? Please?"

"Alright."

"Private Dietrich, your *cat* is sitting on my work."

Franz had been thinking about his conversation with Amos when Edmund's snarl brought him back to reality.

He looked up from his post in front of the prison-cell corridor and smirked when he saw a small brown animal curled on top of a pile of very important-looking papers. Edmund was sitting in front of the fuzzy paperweight, scowling down at the feline as though he hoped to frighten it away with his icy expression.

Dietrich hopped up from his desk and stuttered an apology to his superior officer. From across the room, Sigmund Rahm cackled. If it weren't for Sigmund, Mausefalle the Second (as Franz had been calling the cat in his head) would have been tossed onto the streets long ago given how much he annoyed Edmund. Luckily, Sigmund was an animal-lover, and Dietrich's suggestion that the commandeered feline become their troop's new mascot had been met with enthusiasm from the SS Major.

"Bring him over here!" chuckled Sigmund as Dietrich, still muttering apologies, plucked the feline from

Edmund's papers. Mausefalle the Second, who was entirely unlike the monstrous barn cat that he had been named for, went limp in Dietrich's arms, purring so loud that Hitler probably could have heard him from the Berghof.

"Can't believe you let him keep that thing, Sigmund," grumbled Edmund, grabbing a pen and hastily scrawling a chicken-scratch signature onto a death warrant. "This is an SS troop. We don't need a mascot."

"We don't need fancy uniforms and nice desks either, but they're still nice to have!" argued Sigmund, smiling as the cat was dropped on top of his already-complete stack of documents. No sooner had the feline's rump touched the papers when he leapt from Sigmund's desk and trotted right back to Edmund, letting out an affectionate "meow" and rubbing his face against the flustered *Untersturmführer's* jackboots. Sigmund feigned offense.

"Well! Fine!" cried the Major. "Not the first time I've been spurned by a *muschi.*"

"*Sigmund!*" yelped Edmund, his cheeks turning the approximate shade of the swastika flag behind him. Mueller let out a single guffaw of laughter before a cold look from Edmund made him bite down on his lip and mutter something about checking up on the prisoners. Franz, who tried to maintain a cold facade while he was on duty lest the shield of ice around his heart weaken, found himself smiling as the cat hopped back onto Edmund's papers.

Dietrich removed the feline three more times, but the cat kept returning to the furious Edmund Rahm. Sigmund was howling with laughter as his brother, who could beat a man nearly to death without flinching, refused to even touch the feline and kept ordering Dietrich to get their "mascot" away from him.

Eventually, Edmund submitted. He reached out and

stroked the cat's back. That seemed to satisfy Mausefalle the Second. The troop mascot purred victoriously, licked his paw, kneaded the death warrants, and then hopped off Edmund's desk and trotted to his designated bed: a crate full of pillows and sheets that sat beneath the window.

"I hate that creature," muttered Edmund, and Dietrich knelt by the slumbering cat, stroking his head and softly promising that Edmund didn't mean that.

FRANZ'S FATHER had never bought him a coat. Or gloves. Or a scarf. Amos had provided him with winter wear, which had always been several sizes too small for Little Franz Keidel, but it had been better than nothing. He still had the torn-up gloves he had taken with him on the day he had run away from home. He had never had the heart to throw them out.

So when Franz was taking a short break after they had yanked a family of Jews out of some poor German family's freezing basement, he started to think of how much the Jews had shivered, and he began to think of Amos…

It was getting colder, and Amos needed something warm.

He ambled through the streets, gritting his teeth when he passed propaganda posters commanding Germans to turn in any Jew they found and barely holding in a wince when a few Hitler-Youths gawked at him with reverence. He usually drank in their innocent adoration, but now it felt wrong. If they knew that he wasn't the perfect Aryan soldier...

Hoping to dodge their awe-filled eyes, he ducked into a clothes shop and almost ran face-first into a mannequin bedecked in a black coat. Amos' size, and on sale too.

Franz grabbed the coat and a pair of white gloves. "Christmas gifts for a friend," he chuckled when the nice old shopkeeper noticed that the clothes wouldn't fit the tall SS man. Not a lie. Not a problem.

Amos' smile was worth the ripping and burning sensation that consumed his soul. Food was one thing, but spending money on a Jew? His money? The Reich's money?

The money he had earned by hunting down every Jew except Amos....

He put the thought aside and drank in Amos' gratitude.

"These are brand damn new!" the J—*Amos* exclaimed, pulling on the gloves and rubbing them on his cheeks, turquoise eyes dancing at the softness. "You didn't have to get me these!"

"Look, Amos, I've already given you food and kept you a secret from my comrades. At this point, I've invested too much to have you die of frostbite."

"Ha! Sunk cost, eh Hahnchen? I can live with that! Wow...I don't think I ever owned anything this nice, not even when I was legally still a person. I guess the SS pays well?"

"Not...exactly. I just don't usually spend very much of the money I earn. I don't drink, smoke, and I'm not married or dating, so I save a pretty penny."

"No girlfriend?" Amos laughed. "Come on! The guards at the Ghetto had girls falling all over 'em, and they weren't half as good looking as you!"

Franz let out a nervous chuckle, desperately attempting to suppress the writhing in his gut. "Ah...well. Nothing's ever worked out for very long."

Not for lack of trying. When a few too many of his fellow soldiers had given him the side-eye and teasingly declared that he must have been a queer since he didn't gawk at every good-looking girl he saw, he had tossed himself into the waters.

Thankfully, he knew for a fact that he wasn't queer. Once he actually got to know a few girls, once he started warming up to them, he had found himself actively desiring them. After that, his comrades had stopped calling him a queer and instead started teasing him for being so emotional.

Still, it didn't matter. Those relationships had been pleasant, but none of the girls had been marriage material. They had been nice girls, lovely girls, but for some reason he had known they weren't for him. Perhaps they simply hadn't understood each other enough, and apparently for Franz that was more important than even the loveliest features.

He flushed when he realized Amos had called him good-looking. He was joking, of course.

Wasn't he?

"That's a shame," Amos muttered, and Franz wasn't sure if he liked or feared the gleam in his old friend's eyes. "Their loss."

FRANZ STARTED BRUSHING his hair before he went to see Amos. Brushing his hair and bathing and making sure he still looked good. He hadn't thought of making himself presentable before. What did it matter? He was going to visit a fugitive J—

Amos.

It didn't matter how good he looked, it just mattered that he looked frightening enough, proper enough, that anyone who glanced his way would avert their eyes and mind their own business.

But it wouldn't *hurt* to look good.
It wasn't a problem.

"THIS...IS A PROBLEM."

Indeed it was. A chunk of the wooden roof had rotted away and left the inside of the barn soaking. Fortunately, Amos himself was all right. He and Herr Winkler had even managed to patch the hole by the time Franz arrived. Unfortunately, Amos' little collection of books hadn't survived the rainfall.

"Do you think you can dump this somewhere?" Amos asked, handing Franz a bag full of the destroyed tomes. "I don't want someone to see them. Some of them are banned, and Herr Winkler…"

"You know, the SS has better things to do than go through some farmer's trash," Franz chuckled, nevertheless opening his arms. "I'll take care of it. We collect so many banned books, I'm sure the Rahms won't notice a few more, even if they're ruined."

"Hey, say you ruined 'em, maybe you'll get a promotion."

"Ooooh, you haven't met my boss."

"Thank God."

"*Untersturmführer* Rahm's a menace even for an SS man. That man could give a polar bear frostbite, and he always finds a way to bitch and moan no matter what we do. Bring in a banned book that's in perfect condition? You probably read some of it, you're awful, disgrace to the Führer. You bring in a sopping-wet illegible banned book? Destruction of evidence, we'll never track down their owners now, disgrace to the Führer."

"If he's that awful, why do you work for him?" Amos'

query was delivered in a light-hearted tone, but with a muted note of seriousness.

"Technically, I work for his brother. Sigmund's not as insufferable; he has a good sense of humor at least. I've had worse than the Rahm brothers, let me put it that way."

"I'll bet..." mumbled Amos, turquoise irises glittering even as he grimaced.

Eager to change the subject, Franz looked down at the bag and muttered, "Sorry about your books. What are you going to do now?"

"When you're not here...wait for you to come, I guess. Count stalks of hay?"

Amos sighed and kicked at his big bed of straw. "Boring is good, remember?"

Franz returned to SS HQ and presented the sopping books to Edmund Rahm. The *Untersturmführer* was, predictably, less than thrilled with his underling's finding.

"Do you typically go through every random bag you find on the side of the road?" grunted the *Untersturmführer*.

"It looked suspicious, sir."

"An SS man doesn't rifle through the garbage. Leave that to our informants. Have some dignity."

"Yes, sir..."

"Put it in the contraband department." *Untersturmführer* Rahm gave Franz the key. The "contraband department" was really just a contraband closet, and it mostly existed to keep the valuables that they snatched from Jews away from the greedy hands of the less scrupulous SS men. Gold and silver Judaica, menorahs and jewelry emblazoned with Stars-of-David that would need to be melted down and stripped of their Jewishness before they were sent to the Reich's coffers.

It was more out of formality than necessity that they also stored banned books and Torah scrolls in the closet, and Franz knew for a fact that while Edmund kept careful tabs on every coin and golden trinket they confiscated, he didn't bother doing the same for all the books.

So it was easy enough to toss the wet bag of ruined books into a corner and carefully grab a few that he knew Amos would like.

It was easy.

It wasn't a problem.

The Reich wouldn't even notice.

He was already breaking the law anyway.

Might as well.

The ripping sensation intensified.

Amos' smile was worth it. He took the bundle of books with one arm and grasped Franz's hand with the other, giving it a tight squeeze.

"Thank you so much, Franz," he said, his voice soft and full of joy. Franz felt strange, like the blood in his veins was simmering. He pulled his arm out of Amos' grasp even though he truly didn't want to.

"You really went all out! *Bambi*, hey! I don't know why they banned this. I thought Hitler hated hunting. Oh, and Jack London! And hey, look, *War of the Worlds!* Did you hear what happened when they read this on the radio in America?"

Amos kept talking and talking, glowing as he thumbed through the crisp novels he'd been provided. He babbled on about how HG Welles had done a radio broadcast of his book and the Americans had thought aliens were truly invading earth.

It was nice seeing Amos like this. Healthy, warm,

bursting with life. It was really nice to just watch him talk, watch his eyes sparkle, listen to his voice…

"Hey, Hahnchen! Franz!"

Amos snapped his fingers in front of his friend's face, his bright smile morphing into a snide smirk.

"Eh…what?" muttered Franz, shaking his head and turning scarlet when he realized he'd been so transfixed just watching Amos talk that he'd stopped actually listening.

Amos giggled. "Just tell me if I'm boring ya into a coma!"

"You weren't boring me. I, ah, just…was thinking…"

"About aliens?"

"Sure," Franz snorted. "About aliens."

"Hey, here's a question: if aliens are real, aren't they *übermenschen?*"

"If aliens are real, they're not *menschen.*"

"So if it's a choice between aliens or Jews, you think Hitler would rather deal with aliens?"

"I'll have to ask him next time we meet."

"Eh. Don't bother. I have a feeling I know the answer."

Amos ran his thumb along the spine of the book, his smile dampening, his eyes becoming cloudy as sorrow returned, as he remembered where he was and who he was.

"Hey," Franz said, eager to change the subject, to make Amos' smile return. "If those Americans fell for that silly Welles radio play, they must be really stupid. Or maybe he's just really good at reading. Very convincing. What do you think?"

That worked. Amos smiled. "Well, I've never met an American, so I don't wanna judge them all by their dumbest kin. Probably the latter, though I didn't hear it myself. Bet he wasn't as good a reader as you, though."

"I haven't read anything aloud since we were kids."

"You were really good at it when we were kids, and your voice is much better now."

Franz's cheeks burned. "Ah…you think so?"

"Bet if you read it, you could fool all of Germany. The Nazis would all run into the streets screaming because you'd have them convinced that aliens were about to suck out their blood. Say…for old time's sake…"

Amos gestured towards his couch of straw and plopped down, patting the space beside him and offering his friend *War of the Worlds*. "Do you wanna read it?"

"Read it to you like when we were kids?" Franz snorted.

"Yeah…why not?" The gentle, boyishly hopeful smile that came to Amos' features made it clear he wasn't jesting. Franz's lips thinned as a myriad of *why nots* ran through his head. *Because we're not children anymore. Because it's a banned book, and even if you can read it because you're not Aryan, I'm supposed to be better than that. Because you're you and I'm me. Because…because…because…*

But Amos' smile was wilting and all of those *becauses* faded into white noise between his ears. "All right."

Amos' eyes twinkled like untouched ocean waves. Franz sat beside him, opening the book and reading at a slow, almost nervous pace. The forbidden words filled the moldering barn and made Amos glow.

"'*No one would have believed in the last years of the nineteenth century that this world was being watched keenly and closely by intelligences greater than man's and yet as mortal as his own…*'"

They sat an inch apart. Amos' childish excitement morphed into calm contentment and his eyelids drooped halfway. His head almost touched Franz's shoulder as he stared at the pages with sleepy reverence.

And Franz read on even though he felt strangely ill, like he had eaten something that was far too sweet.

THEY FOUND a family of Jews hiding in an abandoned house. A man, a woman, a six-year-old boy, and a five-year-old girl. The four fugitives surrendered right away. It always struck Franz as odd that Jews, who were supposed to be utterly self-interested beasts, so rarely tried to fight back. Perhaps it was cowardice. Perhaps stupidity, though Goebbels had assured Hitler's devotees that the undesirable Jews were plenty clever. Clever enough to conquer and enslave their racial betters.

"Move, Jews!" Franz commanded, herding the family into a line and preparing to march them out to the truck. The little boy broke from the herd for a moment, reaching for a book that lay on a small cot. Franz grabbed him by his hair, tugging hard.

The boy let out a yelp, and Franz felt his ice-encased heart palpitate. The Jewish child's hair was curly and dark like Amos'. His scream was just like the one Amos had let out when they were little and he had seen a particularly large spider.

This Jew didn't look exactly like Amos, though. Amos had never fixed him with a look that was all at once pleading and hateful.

"Yonah! Please, don't hurt him!" the woman screamed.

Mueller struck her across the face, splitting her lip. "Quiet, stupid Jew-bitch!" he barked.

The little girl clung tightly to her mother's dress, shrieking when she saw her mother bleed. Dietrich winced.

"Don't hurt me! Don't hurt me!" the girl screamed. Mueller might have hit the child, but a sharp command from Edmund Rahm stopped him.

"Just get them out of here!" the *Untersturmführer* ordered. Dietrich grabbed the woman and child, pushing them out of the bunker, away from Mueller. Franz shoved the boy at his father, who grabbed him with paternal tenderness and hastened to follow Dietrich.

Once the Jews had been evacuated, Franz looked down at the book the boy had been so desperate to take with him.

War of the Worlds. Franz picked it up and held it with trembling hands. The cover was different, and it was more worn-down than the one he was reading to Amos.

But it was still the same book. *Different*, but the same.

"Hey," Franz quipped, fighting to sound casual, to sound amused even as his insides were ravaged by a torrent of *that feeling*, that ripping feeling. "Did you know the Americans…they heard a radio play about this book and…"

Edmund Rahm's eyes cut through him like a blade made of ice.

"Ah…never mind…" Franz whispered, and he threw the book onto a pile bound for the contraband closet.

"So…"

"So…"

"Can I ask you a question?"

"Let me guess: why did I join the SS?"

"You know me too well."

"You're too repetitive."

"You're too evasive."

"You really wanna know?"

"Sort of."

"I look good in the uniform."

"Haha! All right, that's fair."

The ripping sensation was overwhelmed by the feeling that his insides had been lit on fire.

REALLY, it was bound to happen eventually. It seemed that Dietrich brought a new toy for Mausefalle the Second to the base every other day. And any day he didn't bring something, Sigmund would present a ball of yarn or a little piece of crumpled paper as an offering to the feline who now seemed to own the SS HQ. And any day *he* didn't bring anything, chances were good someone else would.

The result of all this gift-giving, of course, was that Headquarters, which had once been a model of cleanliness and order, now looked like the interior of a Hitler-loving crazy old cat lady's house. The clash was almost eye-bleeding: cat toys scattered about beneath an SS flag, balls of yarn piled up under a commendation from Heinrich Himmler, toy mice lying on top of a gold-embossed copy of *Mein Kampf*.

Given this state of cat-induced chaos, it was surprising that somebody hadn't tripped over all of Mausefalle's various possessions much earlier. Much to Franz's amusement, that streak was broken by Edmund Rahm.

Franz was the only one who saw it—which was good, because if anyone else had witnessed Edmund's humiliation, the *Untersturmführer* probably would have insisted on punishing the poor cat on principle.

Franz was sitting at his desk, pondering Amos' words, when he heard a girlish squeak and looked up just in time to see Edmund Rahm slip on one of their mascot's bells.

It was a sight that would never fail to bring a smile to

Franz's face when he remembered it, an image that he could summon whenever he needed a laugh: Edmund's severe, icy facade suddenly shattering as he fell backwards. How he flailed his arms and kicked up his legs in a desperate attempt to regain his footing that ended up looking like a too-enthusiastic goose-step. How he let out a shriek which sounded more like the scream of a little Jewish girl being arrested by the Gestapo than any noise that should have come out of the mouth of a valiant SS man.

What Franz wouldn't have given for a recording of that shriek or the tantrum that followed when Edmund landed on his ass and immediately yelped in pain as he found himself sitting on a few more bells.

"God fucking damn fucking cat...in this office...I'm going to kill Sigmund!" snarled Edmund, sitting up and pulling the bell out from beneath his bum. It was a true tribute to Franz's training that he didn't die of laughter right then. The fact that he didn't even chuckle should have earned him an Iron Cross. That he managed to wait until Edmund had righted himself and then strolled past him without even smiling should have been grounds for a promotion.

He was lucky that his workday was almost over because if he'd held in a laugh all day, he might have spontaneously combusted. As it were, he kept quiet until he had punched out and made it to his car, at which point he sat in the driver's seat for ten minutes, laughing until his ribs ached.

He was still smiling when he made it to Winkler's home. Amos noticed.

"What's with that stupid grin, Hahnchen?" giggled Amos in a way that made Franz's heart hurt as much as his ribs and lungs. He told Amos what had happened, punctuating the tale with a cackle as he recounted Edmund's stupid face and his girlish shriek, and it felt good to laugh with Amos about something that had happened hours ago rather than a lifetime ago.

"Wait, so…your comrade kidnapped Winkler's barn cat?" cried Amos. "*That's* what happened to him?"

"Ha! Yeah. And now he's a spoiled little shit."

"That's…" A thoughtful, if somewhat confused look came to Amos' face. "Winkler thought one of you guys scared him off when you came here. He was sad. I'll have to tell him the barn cat's okay."

"He didn't have a name?"

"Nah ah. He was just a barn cat. Wasn't really friendly. Kind of…strange that he liked your comrade."

"Dietrich's…well…he's…gentler than most SS men. Gentler than me."

"Sounds like all of your men spoil the cat, though. Everyone except Edmund Rahm. Hm…strange." Amos' smile dipped, and he grabbed a stalk of hay, nervously fiddling with it.

"Something…wrong?" Franz said. Amos shrugged.

"I dunno. On one hand, your friends are good to that cat. That's good, but those friends of yours, they treat that barn cat better than they'd treat me. It's…wrong. On both counts. It just…I don't know how to describe it. It feels strange."

Franz's smile died on the spot, and he clutched his chest. Oh, he knew full well what Amos was feeling. That strange, confusing emotion that had clawed at his mind the first time he'd realized Jews did not look like the hook-nosed beasts that *Der Stümer* portrayed. When he had seen his first Jew and realized that however inhuman it was supposed to be, it still looked human and talked like a human and joked and laughed and cried and…

He shook his head and banished those thoughts. Amos was ripping a little piece of hay to shreds, his gaze distant, disturbed.

"The barn cat," Franz said, hoping that bringing up an old memory would make Amos' delightful smile return. "We named it Mausefalle. It was my idea. Mausefalle the Second."

That did it. Amos looked up, grinned, and tossed the straw away. "Mausefalle! Oh! You named him after my cat?"

"Your little monster. Mausefalle the Second seems nicer than his predecessor."

"Not to me! Mausefalle the Second tried to break into the barn and rip my face off when I first came here! And he wouldn't even let Gilbert touch him! Little anti-Semite, maybe that's why he took to you Nazis so fast."

"*All* animals hate you, Amos. I don't know why, but the animal kingdom despises *you* in particular."

"I think the first Mausefalle sort of liked me. He didn't *constantly* attack me, just when I grabbed him."

"Amos, he once climbed a tree *specifically* to scratch you. Then he got stuck in the tree and kept trying to attack you *while he was in the tree*."

"I still say that was a botched rescue attempt."

"I will *never* understand why you loved that cat so much."

Amos' bright, nostalgic smile became strangely gentle in a way that made the ripping sensation return, worse than ever.

"Hey…he was mine."

"WELL?"

"Well what, Hahnchen?"

"Well, what did you think of the book?"

"I dunno why it was banned. Seems like Hitler would really like it."

"Uhm…what makes you say that?"

"The ending. Tiny things, little things, little helpless things taking down a superior race. Seems like he could use it as a warning, if he wanted to. What's the term?"

"Symbolism."

"Right. That's what he thinks of me, right? Tiny, powerless, but I'll still wipe him out somehow."

"I…well…that's an interesting interpretation…"

"What did you think of the book, Franz?"

"I…"

"You look like you're swallowing a lime, ha! You didn't like it."

"No…no. I did."

"So what's with the face?"

"It's not allowed. I really *shouldn't* like it."

"You're not supposed to like me either, Hahnchen, but here you are."

"Here I am…"

"Okay, serious question."

"If you ask me why I joined the SS one more time, I swear, Amos…"

"No…uhm…I wanted to know…why'd you run away?"

"You know why."

"Well…yeah. What I meant was…why did you run and…just…run? You didn't even leave a note. I…I really missed you. It kinda hurt. It felt like you just…didn't give a shit."

"No! I mean…no, that's not…I didn't wanna involve

you. You'd...you'd done enough for me. It's not that I didn't trust you or didn't give a shit."

"You know I would have gone with you, right?"

"You...your parents were good. You loved them. You didn't *have* to run away."

"You know I would have gone with you. That's why you didn't tell me."

"...Yeah. I knew."

"Well, I wish you would'a taken me with you."

"I...maybe we should...talk about something else."

THEY CAUGHT A HIGH-RANKED BLACK FOX. Black Fox 120.

They almost didn't because Black Fox 120 was armed with a rusty little pocketknife and Franz was busy. Busy thinking about Amos and what would have happened if he had run away with him.

He wasn't focused, and so the resistance fighter almost managed to bury his blade into the SS man's neck. He managed to slash at Franz's flesh, but the Nazi came to his senses and dodged before the Black Fox could sever an important artery. He decked the Black Fox in the jaw and tackled him, giving *Untersturmführer* Rahm the opportunity to yank a cyanide pill out of 120's mouth before he could bite it and permanently silence himself.

"Dietrich!" snarled the *Untersturmführer*. Franz, who had almost completely forgotten that his younger comrade was with them, looked up and realized that Dietrich was standing only a few yards away, clutching his Luger with both hands. It seemed that the less-experienced SS man had hesitated in the heat of the moment even though he likely would have had a clean shot.

"I-I-I'm s-sorry, s-sir..." stuttered Dietrich.

"If you can't shoot a fucking Black Fox, turn in your uniform!" Rahm snapped, and his usual frostiness had given way to an explosion of fiery anger that was strange as it was terrifying.

"I...I...sorry," Dietrich hiccupped. "I just...we...we're supposed..."

"To take him alive for questioning, but not at the expense of your comrade!" Edmund huffed, fishing for his handcuffs and restraining the Black Fox's hands behind his back.

"I'm sorry," murmured Dietrich. "I'm so sorry, Keidel! I'll shoot next time, I promise."

"Keidel, are you all right?" Edmund asked, and while it seemed that the younger Rahm's voice was physically incapable of softening, he had adopted a tone that was at least verging on genuine concern.

"Fine, sir!" Franz said, pressing his gloved palm over the wound and repressing a hiss of pain. Edmund nodded and bashed the helpless Black Fox's head against the ground.

"You're going to pay for that, filth!" Edmund growled. The Black Fox lifted his face from the dirt, and even in the darkness there was something odd, almost unearthly, about the look 120 gave the *Untersturmführer*. The Black Fox's eyes were blue. Blue, bright, and blazing. They reminded Franz of the willful eyes of his Führer. They held a fire that was frightening and mesmerizing. They were the eyes of someone who could burn down the world if they only had a match.

"Keidel! Focus next time!" A shout from the *Untersturmführer* broke the spell. It seemed that Franz's superior had become the same old insufferably icy Edmund Rahm that everyone knew and hated again. Cold green eyes were fixed on Franz, brimming with disappointment.

"Sorry, sir," grunted Franz, waiting for his boss to turn

his attention back to the Black Fox and flashing Dietrich a small, reassuring smile. The younger SS man sighed as though Franz's silent forgiveness had lifted a hefty weight from his shoulders.

Not wanting to annoy his superior further, he dressed the wound as best as he could on his own. Evidently, he didn't do a very good job because as soon as he visited Amos a day later, the fugitive took notice.

"What happened?!" Amos cried, throwing *White Fang* aside and rushing to the SS man. Franz almost recoiled when his friend put a hand on his shoulder, his fingers grazing the sloppily applied gauze. That feeling, that sensation that his chest was swelling and burning, returned with the ferocity of a lion.

"I...a Black Fox got me," Franz said. "I'm fine."

Amos' hand slipped away. Franz felt unspeakably cold, cold like he did whenever Edmund Rahm regarded him with his pitiless gaze.

"Oh..." Amos muttered, and unspoken questions hung in the air. *What did you do, Franz? Did you kill him, Franz? Do you think he deserved to die, Franz? He was trying to help people like me, Franz...*

A burning sensation overtook him, different and yet familiar. A concoction of anger and something strange and poisonous that rose in his throat and made him blurt out a question that he didn't really want to hear the answer to. "What?" the Nazi snapped. "You think he should have won, don't you?"

Amos didn't hesitate. He looked up, eyes flashing like a sea reflecting a firestorm's glow. "No," Amos said, reaching out and gripping his friend's good shoulder, squeezing it tenderly. "Never."

And Franz knew he meant that.

"I..." Franz mumbled, but then he fell silent because

he couldn't unleash his thoughts. His awful, confusing thoughts.

We're enemies no matter what.

Even if you aren't a Jew like the rest, Amos.

What if something happened?

What if someone else found you?

You'd choose me over a Black Fox, would I choose you over one of my comrades?

The thought was wrenching and all too clear. They would follow a Black Fox to Herr Winkler's. Edmund Rahm would go into the barn this time. Edmund would find Amos...

I'd kill him. I'd kill Rahm...

Killing Edmund Rahm was one thing. Hell, any excuse to kill him would be a gift. What about another comrade? Mueller, Sigmund, the Führer himself...

He realized that Amos' hand was terribly close to the swastika band on his arm. *You can't have both forever. What will you do if you have to choose?*

Amos was so *stupid* for saying such a thing to an SS man and meaning it so much. Franz hated how looking at his bright turquoise eyes was making his heart feel like it was going to combust.

He reached up and pried Amos' hand off of him. Amos frowned for a moment, but his dazzling smile returned when Franz made a decision.

"I'll protect you no matter what, Amos."

HE BOUGHT A SMALL POCKETKNIFE. Amos was clumsy, and there was every chance he might stab himself by accident, but it was worth the risk. He could at least have a chance if an SS officer that wasn't Franz found him one day.

Franz watched with amusement as Amos swung at the air, grinning like he had when they were boys pretending to be valiant knights and wielding sticks as swords. The SS man touched the wound on his shoulder and his smile wilted.

He prayed that Amos would, if he ever needed to use that knife, do a better job than Black Fox 120.

You've armed a Jew. Now you're hoping he kills a comrade. A voice echoed through his head, a voice that sounded like some awful amalgam of his own internal monologue, Hitler's voice, Joseph Goebbels' screech, and his father's bark. Once again, he felt like an altar boy in need of a confession booth.

FRANZ HAD NEVER GOTTEN a gift from his father for Christmas. The area where they'd lived hadn't been a festive place anyway, but his household had been particularly gloomy during the holidays. No tree, no holly, nothing. His father had never even bothered to greet him with a cursory "Merry Christmas" when the day arrived, but that had been for the best. No holiday with Herr Keidel would ever be merry.

Amos had given him more than just a "Merry Christmas." He had always invited Franz to a nice dinner and gotten him some sort of gift. Nothing extravagant. An apple, a bar of chocolate, a top, a set of dice, something he could afford with his meager allowance or something he could get away with stealing from the local variety store. It didn't matter back then. Franz had savored every apple, and he still had the little knick-knacks, the tops and jacks and dice, tucked in a tiny box in his room.

He realized that the Auman family home had also

never had a tree, and their Christmas dinner had been small, and they had never wished one another "Merry Christmas." He hadn't thought too much of it as a boy, for he had been too overwhelmed with gratitude to be curious.

But now he knew why.

"If you were always a Jew, and your family were Jews..." Franz said one day, his voice cracking from their long reading session. "Why did you celebrate Christmas?"

And Amos looked at him, smiling that gentle smile and regarding him with that teasingly tender expression. "For you, of course. I remember my old man was against it, but I wore him down."

Franz swallowed. "That's...why you never complained."

"Never complained about what?"

"That I never got you anything."

"Hey, even if I were Christian, I knew you couldn't get me a gift. You were awful at stealing, and you couldn't buy anything."

No. As a boy, Franz hadn't been able to buy Amos anything.

But he wasn't a boy anymore. He was much better at stealing, stealing from Jews, and his pockets were heavy with money offered by his thieving superiors.

He had to get Amos something. Something special, something to make up for a lifetime of one-way Christmases. Even if Amos didn't himself celebrate the holiday, he deserved to get *something*.

Franz was strolling the streets with his fellow SS men when his eyes wandered to a storefront window, and he found it. The perfect gift: a scarf. A turquoise scarf that matched Amos' eyes.

He ditched his drunk comrades and scurried into the store, yanking it off the mannequin with such ferocity he almost knocked the poor dummy to the ground. He didn't even bother looking at the price.

"This is handmade," said the shopkeeper, a middle-aged woman with a knowing smile, wrapping up the scarf and proudly presenting it to the SS man. "She'll love it."

"Ah...she?" Franz repeated, forcing his eyes to look anywhere else. His gaze fell upon a somewhat gaudy painting of Hitler dressed as a knight that hung behind the woman's head. He bit his lip and stared at the striking blue eyes, his insides burning. He heard the shopkeeper laugh.

"I know that look, young man," she giggled. "Who's the lucky girl?"

Franz's chest burned so awfully he was certain he would turn to ashes. He quickly thanked the woman, keeping his eyes downcast. Hitler the Knight scowled at him from above the shopkeeper's shoulder, and it felt as though the dictator's gaze followed him all the way home.

It was snowing when he arrived at the Winkler farmstead. He knocked on Old Man Gilbert's door and declared that he was going to see his friend, offering the old man a polite "Merry Christmas" before he scurried to the snow-capped barn.

Amos was curled up on a haystack, covered in blankets —no, *entombed* in blankets. Only his ruddy face and one little curled lock of hair peeked out of the woolen cocoon.

"Well, now my gift seems unnecessary," Franz chuckled, presenting the wrapped parcel to the J-

Amos.

Amos the Jew.

The Jewish man's smile was warm enough that the chilly December weather seemed to transform into a balmy spring day. He untangled himself from his blankets, brushed some hay out of his curly locks, and took the gift.

"You really shouldn't…" he started, but Franz held up a hand.

"Don't you dare," the SS man said, and Amos chuckled.

"All right, but just this once. You've given me enough," Amos sighed, gesturing to the jacket and wiggling his fingers to show off his soft gloves. Franz tightened his jaw and shook his head.

"I don't know about that," he whispered. "I hope you like it."

"I have a feeling I'll like it more than Herr Winkler's gift," chuckled Amos, tearing at the paper. "He gave me a Bible, and not even a…oh."

His smile dampened as he uncovered the turquoise scarf. He held it in his arms in a manner that reminded Franz of when they were boys and Amos would reverently gather Mausefalle into a tender and entirely unwanted embrace. Of course, the scarf didn't writhe and scratch, but for a moment Franz despised it even more than he had that old cat.

"You don't like it?" the SS man stuttered, his voice more frightened than he would have liked. Amos shook his head.

"No, I love it…it's *too* nice." Franz saw tears gathering in the Jew's eyes. A smile slowly stretched across Amos' handsome face.

"You deserve more than just a scarf," Franz mumbled.

"A really nice scarf!" exclaimed Amos. "Can you feel this? It's like a cloud! Here, let me…"

He wound it around his neck and stood up, splaying out his arms and querying, "How do I look?"

Franz didn't know how to answer. His chest was on fire. His soul felt like it was being torn asunder.

"N-nice," the SS man said—or, rather, *squeaked*. Amos

did look nice. Very nice, really. Nicer than he had any right to look, being a Jew.

Being a man.

Franz felt like he had been struck by lightning. Amos didn't help when he rushed forward, looping his arms around Franz's neck, pressing his small body against the SS man in all of his swastika-clad glory and whispering a "thank you" that was too quiet and too soft and...

Shit.

Franz realized all too suddenly what was happening to him when the unfamiliar internal sensation that had been tormenting him for too long was complimented by an only slightly more familiar physical reaction. Heat pooled in his cheeks, his chest, spreading through his body, consuming him.

Shit, shit, shit!

He didn't want to, but he pushed Amos away.

"I have to go!" he cried, straightening out his uniform and ducking his head, praying that his SS cap would enshadow his face and hide his treasonous blush.

"What, but you—?" Amos sounded more confused than hurt.

"I have to go, I'm sorry!" Franz was almost screaming now, releasing a yelp of desperation that didn't suit an SS man.

"O-okay, but..."

Franz fled before Amos could say another word, rushing away from the barn, all but leaping over the sheep that were at pasture. He reached his car and almost collapsed on the hood.

He fought to catch his breath, letting the icy air nip at his skin and face. It didn't cool the fire inside of him.

Shit, I'm in love.

CHAPTER FIVE

*S*hit, shit, shit, shit, shit.

The one word, an incantation of aggravation and horror, had been echoing in Franz Keidel's ears for days. Since Christmas, since the last time he had seen Amos Auman.

Amos Auman, his childhood best friend.

Amos Auman, dirty Jew.

Amos Auman, enemy of the Reich.

Amos Auman, who had beautiful turquoise eyes and a smile that melted ice and who had always been there and knew him and made his chest feel like it was on fire...

Shit, shit, shit.

He had always known he was somewhat odd. He didn't become easily infatuated, he had no interest in staring at pin-up girls or pornographic images. He had only ever been sexually interested in a few choice people. People he knew well. *Women* he knew well.

He had thought he was safe. Straight and safe and perhaps just a little too emotionally dependent.

So much for that. He had already betrayed his nation by keeping Amos safe, by feeding him and clothing him and vowing to protect him no matter what, but now…

Now you're a queer in addition to everything else, the malicious little amalgam voice sneered. *A queer, a traitor, a Jew-lover. Might as well join the Black Foxes right now. Throw your SS garment away.*

He shook his head and scurried in front of the mirror, examining himself. Tall, blonde, blue-eyed, Hitler's perfect SS man. Loyal to the Reich except…

Except when it came to Amos.

He gritted his teeth and nearly put his fist through his own mirror. *Amos!* Just thinking about him was making those awful, disgusting feelings arise.

Wrong, wrong, wrong. This was wrong in every way. In love with a Jew. In love with a Jewish *man.* He had fallen so far…even many Black Foxes would have regarded him with disgust.

He looked at his reflection's shoulder, at the blood-red swastika armband. His own cross. The symbol he had sworn his life to. He gritted his teeth.

*This is wrong, this is awful…*Franz thought, touching the swastika. *This is too much…too much…*

And it was pointless anyway. Even if it *wasn't* wrong, even if he would have been willing to act on his terrible urges (and the notion was *oh so tempting*), he knew for a fact that his feelings wouldn't be reciprocated. Amos liked girls. If anything, Amos had always liked girls a little too much. Franz sighed sadly as he remembered the time nine-year-old Amos had loudly declared that Trude Meyer had a nice ass and pinched her buttocks.

Amos had "dated" multiple girls throughout their early years, and even if those "relationships" had been nothing more than hand-holding and cheek-kisses, it was enough for Franz to know his friend would rebuke him if he dared…

He shook his head. Why was he even *thinking* of this? Perhaps it was just a slippery slope. First he simply didn't kill the Jew, then he treated him like a human, then he brought him food, now he wanted nothing more than to wrap his arms around Amos' small frame and…

And nothing! Franz chastised himself. *If anything, you should never see him again!*

But that thought…that thought replaced the fire with a hollow, awful feeling, like he'd plunged his entire body into a frosty lake. Never see him again…it would hurt, it would hurt too terribly.

He loved Amos, perhaps too much. Amos understood him in a way nobody else did. Even if Amos didn't return his feelings, the Jewish man had declared that Franz was more important to him than the Black Foxes, than safety, than himself. Nobody else had ever cared about him that much, not even his comrades in the SS.

Not even Hitler.

And besides, for as much as abandoning Amos would hurt Franz, it would hurt poor Amos even more. It would be cruel. Amos was used to Franz bringing him food and treats and stories and conversation. He hated the thought of leaving Amos alone in that barn, going mad, desperate for someone to talk to. Desperate to be treated like a person instead of a *thing* to either be defended or exterminated depending on one's political views.

And Amos wouldn't even know why Franz had abandoned him.

No. Better to keep visiting him. Franz was an SS man; it was *his* duty to control these base impulses. His lapses so far were manageable, and anything else…any other temptations would simply have to be quashed. For his sake and for Amos'.

He stared at himself, at the scowling SS man before him.

He had never before thought that his own reflection looked so frighteningly foreign.

"You're back!" Amos sounded far, far too happy to see him. Already, Franz knew that this was going to be Hell.

"Yes, I'm sor—*ungh!*"

Amos evidently hadn't connected the dots between the embrace he had given Franz a few days ago and the SS officer's sudden panic. The Jew tossed his book aside, bolted forward, and enveloped his old friend in a tight hug.

Control yourself, control yourself, control yourself, Franz commanded his body as he felt like his every atom burst into flames. Damn Amos for being so *physical* at such an inopportune time. Amos' head rested under his chin far too perfectly and it would have been *so easy* to kiss his forehead or even better to make him look up and...

Nevertheless...it was just a hug. And he had a feeling Amos wouldn't let go until he got some sort of response.

Briefly, quickly, Franz returned the embrace, squeezing only for a moment before pushing his friend away.

Queer Jew-lover, the hateful amalgam-voice whispered.

"You okay?" Amos asked. "You look...mad."

Franz realized he'd been clenching his jaw and relaxed his face, forcing himself to smile.

"Sorry, the Rahms had an assignment on Christmas," he lied with all the ease of a propagandist. Goebbels probably would have been proud if he wasn't currently lodged between Franz's earlobes, screeching at him for being a filthy queer.

"I forgot about it, didn't want them to come looking," Franz said. "I'm...sorry, Amos."

"It's all right," sighed Amos, fiddling with the scarf Franz had given him. "You just…worried me."

God Almighty, his voice was too soft and sweet.

"You were worried about me?" Franz laughed, and he didn't mean for his laugh to sound like a choke, but it did. "*You're* the fugitive Jew here, not me."

Amos' smile stretched and became teasing, sly. It was a smile that was summoning too many awful fantasies. *This is going to be a long visit.*

"Wow," the Jew said, running a hand through his onyx hair and pulling out a few strands of hay which didn't really make him look dirty; it actually made him look quite adorable and *stop it stop it stop it.*

"I think that's the first time you've ever called me a Jew." Amos wrapped the end of his scarf around his wrist tight, too tight, tight enough that the tips of his fingers started to turn purple. "Most of the time you sort of act like I'm not a Jew, like I'm something else."

"You're Amos," Franz said simply. "If anything, you call me a Nazi too much."

"You're not a Nazi?" Amos' query was too hopeful. It hurt Franz to be honest.

"No, I'm certainly a National Socialist," he said. "I just…I'm not perfect."

Far from it. *Queer. Traitor. Jew-lover.*

"Hey, you won't hear any complaints from me," chuckled Amos. "If it makes you feel better, you're Franz."

"Uhm…thanks?"

"You know what I mean! You may be in the SS, I know that, but you're still…you. To me, you're you. Does, uh, that make sense? Probably not."

"No, it makes sense," chortled Franz, fighting with his own cheeks to keep himself from blushing. "I'm me, you're you. Nothing can change that."

"Not even the war," Amos sighed happily. "I'm glad,

you know. Seems like the war changed everything. I was really worried it had...taken you away. I was kinda worried when you left on Christmas and didn't show up. I thought you'd kind of decided to...drift off and leave. I knew you wouldn't turn me in, but I was still...worried. I like having you around, you know. I think if I didn't have you around, it would make all of this so much harder."

Guilt gripped Franz's soul. He had thought of abandoning Amos when the Jew was looking at him with those eyes so wide and wistful and needy.

"Hey, I'm not going to leave you," Franz vowed, and almost by reflex he started to reach out, wanting to grab his friend's hand. He retracted it and instead pressed his palm over his heart. "I promise, okay? I promise I won't just leave you."

He knew he would regret that promise later, but for now, Amos' smile was so worth it that it hurt.

HE TRIED to remember if he had ever been in love before. There had once been a girl named Marlene. He had adored her, but something important had always been missing between them. Being with her had felt like living in a house without a stove or a fireplace: perhaps it could be done, perhaps sometimes it would even be pleasant, but it wouldn't be complete, it wouldn't be a real home. He had let her go before he could waste her time.

He knew he had never daydreamed about Marlene so intensely that his superiors literally had to snap their fingers in front of his face several times to pull him from his fantasies.

"Keidel! Hello?! Keidel, are you alive?"

He was lucky that Sigmund was the one who found

him drifting off instead of Edmund. Edmund would have had him transferred to Antarctica. Sigmund merely chuckled.

"Come on, Keidel! Imagine if the Black Fox tried to escape!" the Major laughed, gesturing to the cells behind him, which Franz was supposed to be guarding. "He could probably just walk right past you and you wouldn't even notice."

"S-sorry, sir," stuttered Franz. The mere thought was so awful it was almost humorous: SS Private Franz Keidel, the man who shook the Führer's hand, letting a Black Fox escape because he was too distracted fantasizing about a Jewish man.

Sigmund Rahm's emerald eyes danced gaily as he waved a dismissive hand. "Ah, it's all right. After the beating we gave him the other day, I don't think that Black Fox is gonna be moving for a while. Still haven't squeezed anything out of him. Heydrich keeps calling, asking us to send him to Jonas Amsel. I keep saying, 'Der Fuchsjäger can catch a Black Fox better than anyone, but I can interrogate a partisan just as well as he can.' Luckily, Heydrich doesn't wanna put too much on his best man's plate. I hear Amsel's sniffing out Black Fox Ten right now, so, you know, bigger fish. At any rate!"

Franz, who had barely heard all of Sigmund's ramblings, felt his heart somersault when the elder Rahm brother leaned in a bit, winked cheekily, and asked, "Who's the girl?"

Franz all but jumped out of his skin, and the snide laugh that Rahm gave didn't help calm him down.

"G-girl?" Franz stuttered, and Sigmund slapped him on the shoulder.

"I knew it!" the Nazi commander cackled. "Don't worry, Keidel. Edmund always has to wake me up whenever I've got a new girlfriend. Hard to think about work when you've got a pretty face on the brain, hm?"

"You've got that right…" grumbled Franz, shame clawing at his chest.

"So, who's the girl? Anyone I know? Maybe that secretary girl Christina, you know she's always staring at you."

"Ah…nobody you know, and it doesn't really matter," sighed Franz. It felt good to be relatively candid. "She wouldn't have any interest."

"Oh, don't sell yourself short, Keidel! You're a good-looking guy and moving up in the world! Just tell her you shook hands with the Führer! She'll be falling all over you!"

Franz hummed noncommittally and turned his face towards one of the cells. There was some light spilling through the bars and into the dark little prison. He could see a shadowy figure curled up on a mat in the corner, dark hair matted with blood. Black Fox 120. He didn't open those frighteningly familiar blue eyes of his.

"Hey…let me guess…she's got family issues," Sigmund Rahm's voice became shockingly gentle. Franz spun around to face him, eyes wide, lips parting as he hastily tried to come up with an answer.

"Ah—family…?!"

"You know what I mean. Family tree might have a blemish or two. Not suitable for an SS man of your caliber. It happens to the best of us…happened to me a few times." Sigmund Rahm's shoulders slumped, and he took off one of his black gloves, gnawing on his thumbnail. That was a habit the Major typically avoided performing on duty, especially in front of Edmund, but Franz had seen Sigmund nibble on his nails once in a while when something was aggravating him. Usually something involving his troublesome niece.

"Himmler's very strict, you know, about who he allows

his SS men to settle down with. Only the best for the best. He's like a father that way, ha!" Sigmund chuckled fondly, but that word, *father*, made Franz's stomach twist. That amalgamate voice returned, Herr Keidel's snarl rising above the rest. *Queer. Traitor. Jew-lover.*

"You know, he's a very nice fellow, and he only wants what's best for his men, but some of his standards can make life unnecessarily difficult. Besides, people with connections, they get to bend the rules all the time. I've even heard one of Hitler's chauffeurs was a mongrel, had Jewish blood, and they named him an honorary Aryan. Ha!"

"That's possible?" Franz muttered, perhaps sounding more eager than he should have. Sigmund even recoiled slightly, as though Franz had shouted.

"Yes, well, I think it was something minor for him," the Major said. "A grandfather or a great-grandfather or something. Not enough for him to be a threat, but enough to bar him from the SS. Still! There may be hope for your lady friend yet. Give me her family tree. Next time I speak with Himmler, I may be able to pull some strings."

"You'd really do that, sir?" Franz muttered. It almost hurt; he liked Sigmund, and Sigmund was trying to be helpful, but he didn't know. If he knew, he certainly wouldn't be so supportive. It almost made Franz feel like he was being lied to even though *he* was the liar.

Sigmund chuckled and slapped Franz's shoulder. "Sure! You're such a hopeless romantic! We've gotta get you paired up eventually! As far as I'm concerned, perfect is the enemy of good. We have bigger problems than good-looking *mischlinge*—err, no offense to your girl."

"I'm sure she wouldn't mind. I'll think about it, sir. Maybe I'll talk to her about it."

"AND YOUR GREAT-GRANDFATHER TOO?"

"Yep."

"And on your mother's side, are you sure…?"

"Hahnchen, I promise you, it's Jews all the way down. German Jews, yes, but that doesn't matter much. You're not gonna be able to convince your superiors that I'm… what was it?"

"An honorary Aryan," sighed Franz, sinking down on his stiff haystack seat and smacking the back of his head against the barn wall. Amos stood a few feet away, stabbing at the air with his pocketknife and regarding his friend with a sorrowful smile.

"I appreciate the thought, Franz," Amos said. "But you're never gonna be able to prove I'm a full human to them."

"You're a full human. Whether you're fully Aryan or not, you're *different*. You have an Aryan soul, you're some sort of mutant among Jews…you're *different*," mumbled Franz, taking off his SS cap and scowling into the hollow eyes of the skull emblem. "I just want everyone else to see that somehow. So you can be safe and get out of this damn barn."

For a brief second, he was tempted to throw the SS cap on the ground, but his fervent loyalty forbade such a brash act of treason. He put it back on his head.

"Hey…" Amos trotted towards Franz, knelt down before him, and *shit, shit, shit* he was far too close now. Amos reached out and grasped him by the arm. Franz felt his skin bubbling, boiling.

"You're really good at…uh…what's the word? Compact…compart…it, uh, means like, separating things off and pretending like they're different when they aren't..." Amos muttered.

"Compartmentalizing," supplied Franz, failing to suppress a smile. Amos giggled in a cluelessly adorable manner.

"Right! That! I know I've said a million times that I'm not different and you just don't believe me, but...I do... *appreciate* that you compartmentalize for me. In the Ghetto, there were so many people whose neighbors and friends, when things got bad, they just threw them away like they meant nothing. When I first saw you in an SS uniform, I was worried you'd do the same. I don't expect you to just change your entire worldview for me, but I...I'm glad you're willing to *bend* it. I'm glad you still...I'm glad I was *that* important to you."

"*Was?*" Franz muttered, no longer fighting his blush. "Amos, you're still important to me."

"Aww!" Amos' cheeks turned pink for a fraction of a second before he released Franz's arm and pulled out his knife. Franz's gut twisted into a knot and the voices in his head went to war. *Dirty queer Jew-lover...you should have kissed him...that's too much, you've already betrayed your nation enough... you might as well try...he doesn't want it...*

"Hey! Are you alive?" Amos' voice silenced the competing thoughts.

"Just...thinking," Franz chuckled. "What were you saying?"

"I was saying that if I'm really important to you," Amos declared, offering his knife to the SS man. "You'll show me how to use this."

"How to use it? It's a knife, Amos. You stab people with it. It's not complicated."

"I've seen you smile behind my back when I'm practicing! I know you think I look ridiculous."

He *did* look ridiculous when he tried to use that knife:

flailing about like a brain-damaged chicken. Heaving a sigh, Franz stood up and drew his own dagger from its sheath.

"All right, fair enough," Franz said. "If I'm going to arm you, I might as well make sure you can wield it properly. Here, your stance is all off..."

And helping Amos adjust his stance was entirely too pleasant for Franz. Even as the voices in his head commanded him to *stop it, stop it dirty queer Jew-lover*, he forced their objections to fade into whispers.

FRANZ'S SHOWERS BECAME LONGER, and he came out of them feeling less clean than when he went in.

He thanked heaven for his apartment's thick walls. Even if he tried to bite his tongue and keep his lustful exclamations quiet, sometimes he was a little too... passionate.

And his neighbors probably would have raised an eyebrow if they heard a male voice yelling for an Amos.

CHAPTER SIX

It was Franz's fault, really. He wasn't thinking. He wasn't paying attention.

It was Amos' fault too, damn him. With every meeting, with every reading session, with every chapter of every book they read, Amos seemed to scooch closer until his thighs were almost touching Franz's.

They had a pattern, Franz and Amos. Franz would turn the page, then Amos, then Franz, and so on. Switching back and forth, taking turns.

But Amos was sitting so close, his head almost resting on Franz's shoulder. The SS man was barely able to *think*, much less read.

But he had to keep reading since reading the book made Amos smile so softly. And so he didn't think. He just read.

"'*Such was the lesson that was quickly borne in upon him. It came hard, going as it did, counter to much that was strong and dominant in his own nature; and, while he disliked it in the learning of it, unknown to himself he was learning to like it. It was a placing of his destiny in another's hands, a shifting of the responsibilities of existence. This in itself was compensation, for it is always easier to lean upon another than to stand alone."*

And then the page ended. And so he reached up and prepared to turn it, but it wasn't his turn. So Amos reached out at the same time and their hands met just above the edge of the page, Franz's hand almost covering Amos'.

It was an accident, but it set him on fire. His body burned, his cheeks flushed. He looked down at Amos, intending to apologize or mutter some sort of excuse.

But Amos met his gaze. Amos's cheeks were scarlet, his turquoise eyes wide and wanting, and his breath had caught in his throat.

Franz realized three things at once.

First: Amos may have liked girls, but he also liked Franz.

Second: Franz had a chance to act out his awful, sinful, degenerate fantasy.

Third: he no longer cared what the disparaging voices in his head said.

To Hell with it.

He curled his fingers over Amos' hand and squeezed, pausing only for a moment to give Amos an opportunity to pull away. When the Jew instead tilted his chin upwards, offering a silent invitation, Franz took the plunge, pressing his lips against Amos'.

If he were to defend himself later—or try to excuse himself—he would have claimed that he was chaste in his approach. Innocent as a virgin schoolboy, really. It was Amos that dropped *White Fang* and deepened the kiss, letting go of Franz's hand and pressing his palms against the SS man's chest.

It was surprising, but certainly not upsetting. Amos was friskier than Franz would have assumed, and that was good, because Franz was utterly clueless. He wasn't a virgin, but his experience extended to bumbling, clumsy efforts with a few girlfriends.

Amos, though...Amos quite suddenly crawled onto Franz's lap, straddling him. Franz broke the kiss with a soft moan. Amos, smiling coyly, turquoise eyes studying Franz in a delightfully malicious manner, reached up. With one flick of his finger, he sent Franz's SS cap flying into a nearby pile of hay.

"A-Amos..."

"Excited?" Amos' tone was low and teasing. He steadied himself against Franz's shoulder and tore the turquoise scarf from his neck, tossing it aside.

"I...ah!" Franz's answer was cut off as Amos leaned forward, kissing the flesh right below his friend's ear and sawing his hips against the German's.

"More?" Amos queried. Any notion of saying *no* was gone by now. Franz could barely remember who or what he was anymore, utterly lost in a haze of want. He put his hands on the Jewish man's hips and bucked against him. Never had he despised his uniform more than he did right then. He was more than relieved when Amos reached up and started unbuttoning his coat, then his shirt, pairing every undone button with a kiss on Franz's neck.

"Amos..." Franz gasped, nestling his face against Amos' neck and, not knowing what else to do, peppering his flesh with hasty kisses. "God...yes...Amos...Amos! A-ah!"

Amos ran out of buttons on the SS tunic and his hand instead trailed down to Franz's fly. He pulled his face away from Franz's neck and flashed a devilish smirk.

"I guess I *was* curious," the Jewish man whispered, climbing off the German's lap and kneeling between his legs. A small burst of clarity struck Franz as Amos started to pull down his pants, then his undergarments. *Is he going to...?*

Yes, he was. And it felt as amazing, so amazing that for a few minutes at least, Franz forgot the war, forgot his uniform, forgot all of his vows, forgot everything except *Amos, Amos, Amos…*

Eventually, it ended. The echoes of pleasure evaporated, and Franz realized three things at once.

First: the barn was fucking freezing.

Two: he was most certainly a dirty queer, because *that*, letting a man do *that* to him, had felt so incredibly good.

Three: Amos had pleasured him, but he had done nothing for his…friend? Lover? What were they now?

Suddenly feeling as though he'd been splashed in the face with cold water, Franz fought to catch his breath and sat up, humiliation burning in his chest when he looked down at his exposed body and undone SS uniform. He realized that Amos wasn't kneeling between his legs anymore. In fact, the Jewish man wasn't even sitting near the hay-couch.

"Amos…?" Franz mumbled.

"Here." The Jew's reply was far too cold for the intimacy of what had just happened between them. Franz looked over just in time to see Amos down a mouthful of water, gargle, and spit on a pile of hay. Self-consciousness made Franz's chest writhe and he hastily pulled up his pants.

"I…ah…I'm not…well…I suppose I should have…but I don't…" Franz stuttered, fighting with his fly, which refused to zip back up. The pleasure had faded completely now, and Franz had never felt more nervous in his entire life.

Something was wrong, he'd done something wrong, but he simply didn't know what he'd done (or what he *hadn't* done that he was supposed to do.) He had fantasized about this for what felt like an eternity, but something about what had just happened rang hollow. When he had envisioned this moment, Amos had clung to him and moaned in his ear and enjoyed it just as much.

But now Amos almost looked angry. He wasn't scowling, he was still smiling, but it was a bitter smile. The same smile he had worn when Franz had returned to the barn after their initial reunion.

Amos heaved a sigh and walked to the other side of the barn, treading as far away from Franz as he could. He leaned his back against the wooden wall, crossed his arms, and slid down so that he was sitting on a pile of moist straw.

"So…" Amos muttered, and his voice was worse than his smile, venomous and defeated all at once. "Now what?"

Franz finally managed to pull up his fly, but he still felt exposed. Naked. "Ah...now…" muttered the SS man. Well, that was a good question. Now what? Could he put his uniform back on and go back to SS HQ knowing what he'd done? What about Amos? Why did he look so...broken?

"I...well...I guess...I'm not…" Franz mumbled, and Amos's smile faltered for a mere second, his eyes flashing.

"You're adorable, Franz, but now's not the time to be *cute,*" the Jew hissed. "Look, I get it, I know how this works. I'd been wondering about it the whole time. I saw how you were looking at me; I'm not *completely* stupid."

"I don't...I don't think you're stupid at all…"

"Good." Amos' tone was bitingly cold now. Colder than the winter winds beating at the barn. "That makes one of us. I was beginning to think you really just cared about our friendship. Stupid me, hm?"

"Amos, what are you talking—?"

"No, no, don't *you* pretend to be stupid now! Like I said, I know how this works. You're *curious.* You had *urges. Bad* urges. *Illegal* urges. Gotta find someone who'll bend over or suck your dick and won't argue because *you've* got all the power. You can experiment all you want on me and you don't even have to worry since if you even *think* someone might find out, you can just shoot me."

"That…that is *not* what I was thinking!" Franz cried, and he might have been offended if the look on Amos' face, a mask of anger concealing a deep pain, wasn't instead making him terribly afraid. "Amos, I would *never*—!"

"Wouldn't you?!" snarled Amos, slamming a fist against the wall behind him. The entire barn trembled. "So you pop in, shower me with gifts, do all this shit…if it's not *that*, then what *is* it, Franz?!"

Amos' voice cracked, and the sound made Franz's heart shatter. A part of him wanted to run, retreat, give Amos the space he was clearly desperate for, but instead he found himself drawn to the quivering Jew. He stood up and shuffled towards Amos, and he hated how the Jew looked up at him with a mixture of fury and resignation.

Amos' hopelessness morphed into confusion when Franz knelt before him, keeping a good foot of space between them.

"Amos…" Franz stuttered, reaching out, but not touching the Jewish man. "I-I'm sorry, I thought that…I thought we were both…I didn't mean…"

He inhaled deeply, begged whatever deity was watching this display to grant him strength, and dared to lean slightly forward, cupping Amos' cheek in his hand. Amos shivered and fear bloomed in his eyes, but Franz felt him lean his face tentatively against the SS man's palm.

"I adore you, that's all," Franz proclaimed. "That's all that was to me. I didn't mean…I'm so sorry, I didn't think you'd feel like you *had* to…I'm so *stupid* and I'm *so* sorry…"

Despite all of his efforts, he'd successfully hurt Amos.

Franz felt like the lowest being on the planet, lower than the most awful Jewish Bolshevik. Lower than a slug.

"I'll leave. I'll just deliver supplies from now on, I'm sorry," Franz vowed, his voice faltering. He started to remove his hand from Amos' face, but the Jew reached up, putting his hand over Franz's. The despair in Amos' turquoise irises had been cast away in favor of wonder.

"No, no, no," Amos whispered. "Don't do that. It wasn't like that, you're not...it's not that I *didn't* want...I just...you...I didn't think you'd actually..."

Franz stopped Amos' bewildered muttering, planting a swift, chaste kiss on his lips. Amos let out a small squeak.

"You'd actually...that," Amos said, and his smile returned, brighter than ever. "Wow...I didn't...wow."

Giggling and absolutely glowing, Amos threw his arms around the SS man. Franz, happily surprised by the change from cold ire to enthusiastic affection, eagerly accepted the embrace and the series of kisses that followed.

"I'm sorry," Amos muttered once he had caught his breath, resting a cheek against Franz's shoulder. "Guess I ruined the moment, hm?"

"It's all right," Franz assured him, gently raking his fingers through Amos' curly hair. "What in God's name gave you that kind of idea anyway?"

Amos stiffened against Franz's chest, squeezing his eyes shut as though he was afraid he might start crying again.

"How do you think I got out of the Ghetto, hm?" Amos murmured, and he might as well have stabbed Franz in the ribcage.

"What happened?" Franz whispered, trying to keep the mounting anger out of his quiet tone. "If you don't want to say..."

"Kommandant took a shine to me. Had a few urges of

his own. He could have been worse, I guess," Amos sighed, nestling almost aggressively against Franz. "He kept *part* of his word. He said he'd spare me and my family if I did what he wanted and kept his secret. He spared me, but not my family. Then again, maybe he just did that because he knew that would hurt more. He always did love hurting me...turned him on..."

"What was his name?" Franz didn't intend to hiss that query in his lover's ear, but he couldn't help it. He didn't even know what this man—if he could even be called that —looked like, but he was already visualizing the many, many ways he could make him suffer.

"Don't." Amos looked up, his eyes wide and morose. "Don't kill him."

"I'll do worse than kill him."

Sigmund Rahm's lessons could go to good use. A few fingernails ripped out, a crushed testicle or two, an eyeball gouged out with burning nails. Oh, yes, that Komman-dant would *wish* he was dead.

"It's not worth it. I don't..." Amos tightened his grip on Franz. "I don't want him getting involved in this, *us*, again. Not again."

"*Us*, hm?" muttered Franz, and he couldn't help but smile when a streak of scarlet bloomed across Amos' face.

"Ah...well, I mean, you *did* say..." Amos started to stutter, but he was cut off when Franz stole another deep kiss.

"I adore you. If you feel the same..."

"I do," Amos whispered. "I really do. I kind of love you."

"*Kind of?*" chuckled Franz, and Amos lightly smacked his chest.

"You know what I meant!"

"I know...then I guess we're...*us*."

CHAPTER SEVEN

T he first few days that passed after Franz and Amos went from friends to *us* were a maelstrom of bliss and bewilderment. The days and nights where he managed to make it to Amos were easily the happiest he had ever experienced.

Not everything changed: they still talked, he still read to him, but the activities they had engaged in as friends had taken on a new intimacy. Even the way Amos called him Hahnchen seemed different, softer. Franz, hardly able to help himself, had taken to calling Amos "schatzi"—my treasure. It tumbled off his tongue too easily. It suited Amos.

It could have been better, of course. For example, if Amos was a woman. An Aryan woman. An Aryan woman with a pure bloodline going back seven generations so they could be together and he could keep working in the SS without feeling like an interloper even though he still *knew* that Hitler was *right*.

Hitler was right. He, Franz, he was just *wrong*.

But being *wrong* with Amos was just so wonderful.

And even though being with him and holding him and

kissing him was *wrong*, and he knew it was wrong, every time he was in Amos' presence, he was flooded with an overwhelming happiness he had never known before. He realized that he had never been truly *happy*. Rising in the SS had filled him with *pride*, with *satisfaction*, but he realized that *happiness* was different.

Happiness was selfish.

Happiness was a drug.

ON ONE HAND, he was certainly a dirty queer.

On the other hand, he wasn't *really* a dirty queer. He had never loved a man before. Amos was just *different*. The exception.

On one hand, loving a Jewish man made him the lowest filth on the planet, a disgrace to the Führer he had sworn his life and soul to.

On the other hand, Amos was Amos. And really, if he was going to fall in love with a Jew, it was probably better to love a man rather than a woman. At least this way, he wouldn't accidentally make more Jews.

On one hand, the amalgam voice had stopped screaming and had started whispering, its insult now restrained to one word. *Hypocrite, hypocrite, hypocrite.*

On the other hand…

On the *other hand*…

Franz didn't believe in God, and he didn't believe in an afterlife. Nobody was watching. His sin was confined to the four walls of the barn, confined to Amos. He wasn't hurting the Reich. He was still serving it as well as he could in his capacity as an SS man.

It's different.

He's different.

It's not a problem.

He comforted himself by remembering Ernst Röhm. Hitler's old party comrade, the head of the Brownshirts, one of the original National Socialists, a man who had built up the Reich and acted as a bulwark of the German revolution.

Röhm had been a homosexual. Brazenly homosexual. But he had also been a National Socialist.

Of course, Hitler had eventually had him killed.

Still, Röhm should have just kept it quiet. There wouldn't have been any problem if he'd just been subtle and quiet and secretive like Franz.

And regardless, Ernst Röhm the homosexual had still died a National Socialist.

So really, Franz figured he wasn't *that* much of a hypocrite.

"Uhm…"

"Every time you begin with 'uhm,' Franz, I swear…"

"Should we have a word? In case I am hurting you."

"Sure. The word is 'ouch.'"

"I'm serious, schatzi…I *really* don't want to hurt you."

"The word is 'owieowiethathurt.'"

"*Amos.*"

"The word is 'mood-killer,' because that's what you are right now."

"Ugh, I don't know why I bother."

"Wait, I like this train of thought. Maybe we should

make it something that's a *real* turnoff for you, so it'll make you stop right away."

"Amos…"

"Torah?"

"*Amos…*"

"Hanukkah?"

"Amos!"

"Stalin?"

"Ugh! Now *you're* a mood-killer!"

"Stalin it is, then!"

AFTER EVERYTHING AMOS had been through, it almost felt wrong to screw him in the barn. Pleasurable, certainly, and Amos didn't seem to mind, but to Franz it was dehumanizing. He wished they could have had a bed, a real bed instead of just a pile of hay.

Amos deserved better. Animals got screwed in barns, and while Amos was worse than an animal to the Reich, Franz knew better. Amos was *different*.

AMOS PROBABLY THOUGHT that his love would soften SS Private Franz Keidel. Make him better even if it didn't redeem him.

But really, it only made Franz worse.

He became a better SS man during the day. He had to. To atone for the sins he committed every time he visited Amos. He had to serve his Reich more ardently to make up for his personal exception.

He became a better Nazi.

He was worse to the Jews they arrested who reminded him too much of the haggard Jew he loved. He was worse to the prisoners who regarded him with scowls too similar to the one Amos had given him when he'd thought Franz only wanted to use him. The flickers of humanity that existed in his enemies became inescapable, impossible to ignore, and whenever he noticed them, it would make him feel sick.

He would see Amos in the undesirables he abused and hate himself for hurting them. Then, desperate to keep that fire of self-hate from melting his heart and burning his soul to cinders, he'd force it outwards. Force it to burn his foes instead. Then, for a moment, he would feel clean again. Pure.

It's different, he'd assure himself as he beat them, screamed at them, held them down and let Sigmund Rahm scald their flesh with cigarettes.

He felt like a priest who, burdened by the sins known only to him and a few altar boys, declared a crusade.

It made him feel better until he went back to the barn and saw Amos' bright smile and his adoring eyes. Franz would wonder what Amos would think if he saw the fruits of his lover's holy war.

Hitler was right. And he had to be right.

Because if he was wrong, then Amos wasn't just an exception.

If Hitler was wrong, then Franz was not a knight who had strayed from the path of righteousness. If Hitler was wrong, then Franz was a murderer.

And if Hitler was wrong and Amos wasn't the exception and Franz was a murderer, then Franz wouldn't deserve Amos.

And that…that would be worse than anything.

THEY CAPTURED an escapee from one of the local concentration camps.

He had a pink triangle sewn above his heart. The brand of a homosexual.

He had black curly hair, and if his eyes had been turquoise instead of sapphire, he would have looked too much like Amos for Franz to bear it.

It's different. He forced the assertion to echo about his mind as Sigmund Rahm tried to pin the prisoner down. The queer man was small, small like Amos…

It's different. More forceful, more desperate, he tried to assuage his soul. The man with the pink triangle was small, but he was shockingly strong. Even pitted against a well-fed, well-trained SS officer, he managed to hold his own and keep himself from being tied down to the little blood-splattered chair.

"Dietrich, help me with this degenerate!" the Major snapped, and Franz glanced to his side. He and his younger comrade had been stationed on either side of the interrogation room door, ordered to stand guard in case the prisoner made a break for it. Dieterich's hand, which had been hovering near his sidearm, began to tremble.

"I…" the younger man said. Franz, sensing Dietrich's fear, stepped forward.

"Major, I'll help," he volunteered, but Sigmund regarded him with irate green eyes, as though he were a star pupil raising his hand for the hundredth time in science class.

"No, Keidel, Dietrich needs to pull his weight! Dietrich, *now!*"

Franz tightened his jaw and tried to summon a shield of ice to surround his soul as he stepped back. Inhaling sharply, Dietrich obeyed Sigmund, shuffling towards the prisoner and grabbing his wrists. The younger SS man kept his eyes averted from the prisoner's bruised face as he tied him down. The man with the pink triangle started sobbing, an awful sound that echoed about the small space.

"Shut up!" Sigmund slapped the prisoner across the face. One tooth flew from his split lip.

It's different.

He tried so hard to ignore the ripping sensation in his gut.

It's different.

"Dietrich, grab those pliers."

"Sir…"

"You need to learn how to interrogate a prisoner."

Dietrich's eyes glistened with fear. Pink-Triangle started writhing, screaming, begging for mercy. Every desperate shout chipped away at the thin layer of ice Franz had formed around his heart. The fire of self-loathing burned in him. He tried to banish it, fling it back at the prisoner, but he couldn't. The man looked too much like Amos. It was impossible to hate him.

But Dietrich was shaking, and no matter how agonizing it would be to torture someone who looked like the man he loved, Franz felt a brotherly obligation to save the boy from such a gristly task.

"Sir, let me…"

"*Franz, I said no,*" Sigmund snapped, his eyes blazing as he gave Dietrich a shove towards the tool table. "Dietrich, pliers, ***now! Follow orders!***"

Dietrich did, though it seemed like he barely drew in a

breath as he picked up the rusted instrument and brought it back to the Major.

"Here's how this will work," Sigmund snarled, leaning above the prisoner. "You will tell me how you escaped. Who helped you? Who have you spoken to?"

"N-nobody h-helped me," Pink-Triangle sobbed, barely able to get out a word as he struggled to breathe. "Please, I-I w-won't d-do a-anything b-bad ag-again, I swear to the Führer…"

Slap!

Dietrich winced. Another tooth went flying, landing near Franz's feet. *It's different.*

"Disgusting queer!" snarled Sigmund. "You have some nerve speaking his name! That will cost you a fingernail! Dietrich!"

"Sir…"

The Major looked down at the younger man, opening his mouth. Franz readied himself to leap forward and beg for the duty, but it seemed that seeing Dietrich's placid face made Sigmund feel a stab of pity. Not for the queer. No. Of course not. But no doubt the Major realized that rushing this sort of lesson would only traumatize his underling. He liked Dietrich too much to push him any further.

The Major offered the younger SS man a small, almost apologetic smile and reached out his hand. "Give it here, Dietrich," he said. "I forgot you've never been in the room before."

Dietrich's shoulders relaxed. "Yes, sir," he said, handing him the pliers. "Thank you, sir."

"Can't avoid it forever, Dietrich. Next time, I'll expect you to be tough," Sigmund said, practically shouting over Pink-Triangle's wails. The Major smirked, held up the pliers, and clicked them almost playfully.

"For now, watch and learn."

Dietrich did. So did Franz. One fingernail was ripped from the man's left hand. The scream should have been pleasant, the sound of an enemy getting what they deserved.

But he sounded and looked like Amos.

It's different.

Dietrich flinched as the Major threw the nail aside and it landed near his polished jackboot.

It's fine.

Mercy. The queer begged over and over for mercy. Mercy he would never be offered. An SS man wasn't supposed to show mercy to any undesirable.

Amos is different.

Another nail. Franz's ears ached.

It's different.

He could feel Dietrich's gaze upon him. His chest burned. He looked down, shutting his eyes and hoping that he could feign boredom.

It's different.

He could barely hear the man screaming through the sound of his own pulse pounding in his ears.

It's different.

The denial and his own heartbeat drowned out the howls. The cacophony in his head gave him the opportunity he needed to harden his heart again.

It's different.
He's different.
He's Amos.
Don't think about this.
Don't think.

"Hey, what do you think of kids?"

"Uh...kids?"

"Yeah, kids. Like, raising kids."

"You and me? Amos, I hate to point out the obvious, but that's impossible."

"Oh, I'm sure there will be a lotta orphans running around after this is all over with."

This. The war. How did Amos think it would end? To Franz, a victory for Germany was the only possibility.

"They'll need a good home. And I'd really like to be a father, but only if I can become one by...you know...helping some little kid that doesn't have anyone else. We could take a few in, get a nice house somewhere private, and raise 'em well. Be a real family like everyone else. It would be nice, don't you think?"

It *would* be nice.

But it would never be possible. Germany would win, and there would be no sanctuary. No private place where they could raise a bunch of little orphans and be a family.

But Amos sounded so wistful and hopeful, and Franz couldn't possibly break his heart by telling him the truth.

"It would be nice," he confessed, and that was all he could say without lying.

CHAPTER EIGHT

T he honeymoon ended one beautiful day.

As usual, Franz approached Winkler to announce that he would be visiting Amos. He realized by the severe look on Gilbert's face that there was a problem.

"Sir, Herr Winkler, did something happen?" Franz queried, his heart racing as he prayed to a deity he was certain didn't exist. *Not Amos, please don't let anything happen to him...*

The old man sucked his teeth and swayed slightly, his aged eyes flitting nervously to the swastika on Franz's arm. He took in a shuddering breath, seemingly steeling himself before he declared, "You need to leave, and you need to take the lad with you."

Franz blinked twice and suddenly became acutely aware of the Jesus portrait that was eyeing him from Winkler's foyer. "I...what? I don't know..."

"I'm old, Herr Keidel, but I'm not deaf," Gilbert said, his wobbling voice becoming stronger with anger. He pointed a gnarled finger in the direction of Amos' barn and hissed, "I've heard what you two have been doing in there."

Franz felt the blood drain from his cheeks. "Look," he said, trying to keep himself from stuttering. "I'm sorry, I didn't mean to disrespect your home..."

"I can't condone that, Herr Keidel. I'm a man of God."

"I know, but...listen. I'll stay away from now on, I'll only come to bring supplies," Franz said, reaching out almost desperately. The old man recoiled and shook his head.

"Absolutely not, no, I can't accept that."

"But we won't...we won't do anything ever again, you won't have to worry!"

"I agreed to protect the son of my old friend, to protect a child of Israel," Winkler whispered. "I never agreed to protect a homosexual. Frankly, if his father knew what was going on between you two, he'd agree with me completely."

"His father's dead," snarled Franz, fury forcing him to do something stupid: he reached down and touched his sidearm. "I promise you'll be dead too if..."

"*If.* Are you going to shoot me? Fine, but then he'll be found and sent to a camp anyway," Winkler snapped, reaching up and grasping at the cross dangling from his neck. "I'm trying to be reasonable. I'm giving you a chance to take him, but if you won't, I won't let him stay here."

"'Won't let...?' What, are you gonna call the SS on him?!" snarled Franz, stomping one jack-booted foot on the "Welcome" mat, making the small house shake. Winkler stumbled back, lifting up his arms over his chest as though he was trying to shield himself from an oncoming attack.

The old man didn't say a word, but Franz knew from the look in his eyes that the answer was *yes*.

It wasn't surprising. Queers were hated by the Allies and the Axis, by atheists and believers, by Nazis and communists, even the Black Foxes didn't actively try to help them. Despising homosexuals was a universal trait. Winkler wasn't special in that regard.

And killing the old man wouldn't do Amos any good. It would be a waste of time and bullets.

"Fine…fine!" Franz snapped, slamming his fist on the door and pointing a gloved finger in Winkler's face. "We'll go! But if Amos gets hurt, old man, I'll come back here and kill you."

The old man bit his bottom lip and glanced over his shoulder at the picture of Christ. Inhaling deeply, he quietly proclaimed, "May God forgive you, son."

"Go to Hell!" snapped Franz, spitting on the old man's chest, aiming for the cross but instead hitting his shoulder. Winkler let out a small yelp and hastily scurried towards his bathroom, as though he feared Franz had infected him with an awful disease.

Franz stomped away from the house, nearly kicking the hens that ignorantly trotted after him as he threw open the barn door, letting the birds stream into Amos' hiding spot.

"Amos, get up!" Franz cried, whipping the large blanket aside and pulling his lover from his bed of hay. Amos, dazed, grasped Franz's arm and dusted the stalks of straw out of his dark hair.

"Franz, you scared the hell outta me. You didn't announce—hey! What?!"

Franz started to yank the Jew towards the open door. "We have to leave, now!" he declared.

"Is it the Gestapo!?" squeaked Amos, clinging to his lover's arm. Franz stopped right at the threshold of the barn, grunting in ire as a few hens started harassing Amos, pecking at the Jew's ankles.

"No, schatzi…" Franz sighed, barely repressing the urge to punt one of the damn birds as a useless way to let out his anger. "Winkler heard us. Heard *us*."

"Oh…*oh*…." Amos' cheeks turned red; his eyes became round and frightened.

"Hey, hey, it's all right!" Franz insisted, grabbing Amos's face and pressing his forehead against his lover's. "It's all right! I promised I'd protect you, didn't I? You trust me, don't you?"

"Of course," Amos said, reaching up and grasping Franz's hands.

"Then come on. Just do what I say, I'll take you somewhere else…"

"Wait!" Amos broke away from Franz and ran to one pile of hay, gently shooing a few curious hens out of the way as he pulled *White Fang* from the heap.

"Okay, let's go," Amos said, holding the book close and briefly touching his scarf before grasping Franz's hand. "I don't have anything else."

Franz was happy he had bought Amos new clothes, clothes that didn't bear the telltale yellow star. The Jew could sit in the car without immediately drawing attention. He looked groomed enough that a casual observer wouldn't assume he was a fugitive Jew, and if anyone bothered to take a closer look or ask for his papers…well, Franz could probably smooth-talk his way past at least a few checkpoints.

Amos settled into the passenger seat with a strange expression, somewhere between fear and wonder, as though he was about to be beaten to death by a unicorn. "Hm…" the Jew mumbled, running his hand along the control panel of the car and grinning impishly as he played with the window crank.

"Amos," Franz sighed, and despite the agitation and anger consuming his heart, he couldn't help but give his lover the slightest of smiles.

"What?!" giggled Amos. "Never been in a car before. Not really, anyway. When the Gestapo came for us, they tossed us in the back of a truck. That was awful, but this…" He leaned back a bit and winked at Franz. "This is stylish."

"Wonderful, at least I can *stylishly* smuggle you somewhere safe, schatzi," grumbled Franz. "You're remarkably optimistic, you know."

"Gotta be, or else I'd be dead already," Amos sighed, glancing almost woefully out the window, at the barn he had called home for far too long, at the farmhouse where Gilbert Winkler lived. Franz saw the old man peeking at them through the window. The SS man viciously slammed his foot on the pedal and started driving away from Winkler's property.

"Old bastard. Hope he burns," hissed Franz, and Amos fixed him with a gaze that could best be described as that of an affronted kitten.

"Don't say that, Franz," Amos begged, gingerly touching Franz's shoulder.

"Don't defend him, Amos!" huffed Franz. "He was willing to turn you in for this, he…"

"He didn't have to take me in *at all*, but he did," Amos said, craning his neck to steal a glance at the rapidly vanishing farmstead. "I'd be dead long ago if he hadn't done that. I'm grateful to him, regardless of what he did just now."

Franz felt his boiling blood cool as affection settled on his heart. He clicked his tongue and shook his head. "Optimistic…" he muttered.

"Believe me, my situation could be *much* worse," Amos muttered, and Franz thought of the man in the pink triangle, of his bruised face and his screams…

"I'm aware of that," Franz murmured. "As it were, I think there's a way we can make do, at least for a while."

"Are…you gonna take me to your place?" Amos queried. Franz shook his head.

"My place is in the city, an apartment. Too many eyes, too many neighbors. You'll be caught in a day."

"Okay, well…where are we going then?"

Franz tightened his grip on the steering wheel.

THE KEIDEL FAMILY farm was about two hours away from Franz's workplace. Three hours if you factored in traffic. Three-and-a-half if you factored in traffic and all the checkpoints. Four if you encountered traffic and the checkpoints happened to be staffed by soldiers who were being particularly anal about papers.

Fortunately for both Franz and Amos, they traversed the roads at an opportune time. There was traffic but no anal checkpoint guards. In fact, the guards seemed exhausted and eager for any excuse to wave a car through as quickly as possible. Franz only had to flash them a smile, show off his uniform, and give them his SS documents to prove he was actually a member of Hitler's elite guard. The low-ranking soldiers manning the checkpoints didn't check Amos' papers or even ask who he was. Franz, the driver, was a bona fide SS man. That was enough for them to assume all was well and official.

It wasn't exactly an *easy* drive. Every checkpoint still brought about rapid heartbeats and held breaths. Every time they passed through, Amos would let out a loud groan like the checkpoint had been some sort of magical creature that had stolen five years of his life. By the time they reached Franz's childhood home, Amos looked absolutely exhausted, like he'd just run all the way from Winkler's farm to his new hiding place.

"I take back all my optimism," the Jewish man moaned, eagerly scrambling out of the car and taking a great gulp of fresh air. "Cars are moving prisons of pain, and I never want to get in one again."

"Maybe you'd like a convertible better," Franz quipped, following his lover out of the vehicle. "Wind in your hair...I think you'd like that..."

It was a pleasant thought for Franz too: driving through the countryside, watching Amos lean out as far as he could, maybe laughing at him when he inevitably swallowed a bug by accident. It would be nice. Romantic even. Too bad it could never happen.

"Oh...we're *here*..." Amos, having recovered from his car sickness, had straightened up and finally realized where he was. The Keidel house had never been beautiful, but the years of abandonment had turned it into a ruin: windows were broken, paint was peeling, rust covered the gutters, tiles had fallen off the roof.

"You...still...uhm..." Amos stuttered. "I...I know your old man passed away...but....uhm...I didn't know you still owned it."

"Bank tracked me down. I think they were afraid to try and rob an SS man of his family estate. I thought of selling it, but it's such a shithole. I figured it wouldn't be worth the effort," Franz sighed. "Figured I'd just let it rot. We're lucky I didn't just give it away. It's not a perfect hiding place, but it's better than nothing. This whole place is practically a ghost town anyway. I doubt anyone will notice you crawling around here."

"And if they do, they might just think *I'm* a ghost," chuckled Amos, his tone almost desperate as he tried to soothe Franz's obvious anxiety.

"Haha! Actually, from what I hear, the neighbor kids are always saying they see ghosts over here. Probably just kids being kids, but they've reported it so often that if they see you and tattle, it'll be a crying-wolf situation. I doubt they'd send anyone to investigate."

"Kids...neighbors..." Amos's gaze shifted to a farmhouse in the far distance. The former Auman homestead was miles away, but Franz and Amos could see little dots flitting about in the grass. Amos could hear the happy squeals of children enjoying their stolen land.

"Amos...schatzi..." Franz put a hand on his lover's shoulder and started to steer him towards the house. Amos tightened his grip on *White Fang* and heaved a shuddering sigh.

"It's okay," Amos insisted, even though Franz knew it wasn't. "At least someone's enjoying it."

The Jew smiled softly and perked up his ears, as though listening to the distant giggles was somehow giving him strength. Franz shook his head and squeezed his lover's shoulder.

"Optimist," he whispered. "Let's hurry before someone spots you."

They rushed inside and were almost immediately assaulted by a miasma of dust that rose into the air as Franz flung the front door open. Franz hacked until he was certain he was about to cough up a lung, but Amos inhaled the dust bunnies with a gusto.

"It's nice!" he cried. "You know, I realize I've never actually been in here."

Franz blinked the blinding cloud of dust out of his eyes and the vision that greeted him was at once painful and somewhat comforting.

His father must have sold almost everything he owned before he croaked. The Keidel household had never exactly been well-furnished, but now it was almost empty.

No kitchenware, no carpets, no paintings, no logs in the cobweb neighborhood that was the fireplace. Even Herr Keidel's old olive-green cozy chair was gone. There was an unfamiliar floral couch that looked like Herr Keidel might have grabbed it off the side of the road, one little stool, and a small nightstand that rested before the couch like a makeshift table.

"*This* is nice to you?" Franz coughed, searching the old broom closet and noting with not a small bit of satisfaction that the broom he had once used to sweep the house was also gone.

"I was living in a *barn*, Franz!" laughed Amos, plopping down on the couch and somehow inhaling the tornado of dust that flew off the frayed cushions with nary a sneeze. "And before that, I was in a little apartment with three families! *Three!*"

"In the Ghetto, you mean," Franz said, finding an old, ragged blanket in one of the closets and quickly hanging it over the broken window. He would have to board it up later.

"The Ghetto made the barn feel like a luxury hotel, and compared to the barn, this is a palace!" giggled Amos, putting his arms behind his head and his feet up on the couch's armrest. "I feel like a prince!"

"Well...I'm glad you're happy," sighed Franz. Amos' smile wilted as he sat up and reached for his lover.

"Hey, Hahnchen," Amos said, gesturing for him to come over. Franz finished fastening the makeshift blind in front of the window and then scurried to Amos' side, grasping his hand and offering him a gentle smile.

"Don't say anything, schatzi," Franz begged. "It's fine."

"I don't want to..." Amos muttered, squeezing the German's hand, and Franz chuckled.

"Honestly, it's fine. I avoided this place for too long,"

Franz assured him. "It…it's so empty, it doesn't even feel like the same house I grew up in. It's like a shell. Like a completely different place. It's…almost nice."

It *was* nice, actually. Being here, seeing that his father's ghost wasn't stalking about, seeing that he was really *gone*. In his absence, the house was nothing more than a blessing, a castle for Amos.

"Hey, let's see if he kept my old bed," Franz said. "You've been sleeping on straw far too long, you'll never get it out of your hair."

He reached into Amos' onyx locks and plucked out a stray strand of hay, eliciting a giggle from the Jewish man.

"A real bed! That would be nice!" Amos agreed eagerly, letting Franz yank him off the couch and lead him by the hand down the hallway to his old bedroom. They quickly found that it was completely barren except for a rusted twin-size bed frame, a broken lamp, and a feather duster that had clearly lost the war against the debris of Keidel Farm.

Fortunately, they peeked in Herr Keidel's old room and found that not only was the bathroom clean save for the obligatory layer of dust, but there was a bed. Well, a mattress. No frame, just a king-size mattress laying on the floor. No blankets, no sheets, no pillows.

Nevertheless, Amos looked at the pitiful arrangement like it was a throne. He glanced at Franz as though to ask for permission to indulge. When Franz chortled and waved for him to do as he wished, Amos released his lover's hand and collapsed face-first onto the mattress, unleashing a sigh.

"Happy?" chuckled Franz, covering his mouth and waiting for the cloud of dust to clear. Amos, still face-down, nodded.

"It feels like a cloud. It's almost *too* soft," Amos said,

his voice so muffled by the bed that it almost was indecipherable. He rolled over and beamed at Franz.

"I'm almost glad Gilbert kicked me out," he giggled, and Franz felt his stomach sink.

Perhaps it was more comfortable than the barn, but it was going to be difficult. Franz would have to drive many hours to visit. He would have to plan ahead to make sure Amos would be all right during the days when he simply wouldn't be able to make time. He would have to come up with some kind of excuse if someone asked where he was driving to so often…

"Hey." Amos's soft voice dragged him from his thoughts. The Jewish man had scooted over and was patting the space beside him.

"Come lie down," Amos said, not precisely ordering him to do so, but speaking with the forcefulness of a mother commanding a sick boy to get out of the cold. Franz, who usually couldn't resist Amos but was far too stressed to even think of intimacy right then, shook his head.

"Not now, schatzi, I…"

"I don't want to screw right now, Hahnchen. I'm tired too," giggled Amos. "Just lie down with me for a moment. I can tell you need some rest."

"I should probably get supplies…"

"Later. C'mon…" Amos crawled to the edge of the mattress and reached up, grabbing Franz by the hand and almost dragging him down. Franz submitted, lying down with Amos tucked under his arm, his mind still buzzing with anger at Winkler and…

He tightened his grip on Amos' shoulder and sighed, shutting his eyes. *Later,* he thought. For now, this was nice. He knew it wouldn't last, and so he decided to enjoy it.

CHAPTER NINE

I t was exhausting. Balancing his SS life with Amos had been difficult enough when Winkler had done half the work for him, but now he was on his own, salvaging food and water and razors and everything else Amos needed.

Then there was the grueling drive both ways, which meant that he arrived at Amos' new hideout bone-tired and returned to work a husk. Sigmund increased Franz's caffeine rations when the Private fell asleep during a particularly loud interrogation. Dietrich offered to cover a few of his shifts if there was something wrong. Edmund Rahm commanded him to get his act together *or else*.

It was exhausting, but it was also strangely pleasant. He would arrive at the house that no longer brought back memories of wanting to hurl himself from the roof, a house that now meant Amos and love and pleasure instead of beatings and hurt and pain. He would stumble through the front door with all the weariness of a husband who had been away at an arduous job, and it was so domestically nice to have Amos greet him with a hug and kiss.

It was delightful to embrace his lover at the threshold and bury his face in Amos' scarf-clad neck. It was easy, too easy, to imagine how wonderful it would be if this could be permanent. He could practically hear the pitter-patter of tiny feet as all the little orphans Amos would adopt ran to greet him.

Then, of course, Hitler's voice would remind him of who he was and what Amos was. *That won't ever happen. Traitor. Queer. Hypocrite.*

On one hand, this arrangement was simply unsustainable. Eventually, something would happen. Rahm's troop would be reassigned, or the neighbor kids would get too nosy, or Franz simply wouldn't be able to make the long trip anymore (the fear of what he would do if his car broke down made it even more difficult for him to sleep even when he had time.)

On the other hand, it was so, *so* nice to be alone with Amos. To sit on the couch together and read from the books he stole from the contraband closet, to talk and laugh together.

Being in a house instead of a barn made it feel like their relationship was real, real and human and built on love. Amos would joke about cooking for Franz next time he arrived ("If I can just get this damn stove to work!") and something about the idea was nice, romantic even. It would have been lovely to share a real meal with him. It would have been nicer to take him out to a restaurant and treat him, but still...Franz had to see the good in what they had. He had to be an optimist like Amos.

Amos seemed so, so happy in the husk of a house. Being able to sit on a couch and sleep in a bed (well, a mattress) like a real human being seemed to fill him with so much joy that it was almost contagious. It was simply impossible for Franz to enter Amos' little kingdom and watch his lover gush about how he had stitched up a few of the holes marring "their" couch (because nothing in the house was his, it was all "theirs") and not feel his soul glow as it soaked up all of the Jew's happiness.

On one hand, the fact that he was enjoying this cruel imitation of a home life so much was pathetic. Every second he spent at that house was wonderful, but it made the inevitable return to his SS duties almost unbearable. He would stand guard over whimpering prisoners, watch beatings, watch executions, participate in executions, all the while knowing that Amos was waiting for him with a smile and a kiss.

And he would have rather been with him, with Amos, than standing guard. And that was wrong. So wrong. Being a queer Jew-lover was bad enough if it was a hidden part of his life. But if it *became* his life...

On the other hand...well, he knew from experience that the neighbors were too far away to hear shouting. And there wasn't a lot of furniture left in the house, but there was enough.

And he hadn't been wrong before. Sex in the barn had been a raw affair: affectionate, yes, but also dehumanizing. He wouldn't have even called it lovemaking; it was always a hasty effort filled with as much fear as it was pleasure. Franz and Amos had always been very careful not to even take off all their clothes when they did it, at most only pulling their pants around their ankles, always prepared to dress quickly if they were interrupted. Franz only realized when they were finally in a house, in a bed, able to act like lovers instead of animals, that he hadn't even seen Amos fully naked yet.

Amos didn't disappoint.

On the other hand, he almost wished he would. Because fucking a Jew was one thing, but making love to one and then holding him afterwards and stroking his cheek and then waking up in the morning knowing he would have to go to work and beat a Jew with the same hands he had just…

It made him feel like his skin was being eaten by ants. He felt dirty. And no amount of gritting his teeth and mentally declaring that *this is different, it's fine, it's not a problem* was making the feeling that his soul was being broken apart go away.

REALLY, they were lucky Amos hadn't gotten sick sooner. Franz had worried that all the dust he was breathing in freely would cause him to catch tuberculosis or something, but apparently Amos' immune system was stronger than one would have assumed given how fragile he looked.

Still, it wasn't nothing. Poor Amos was barely conscious: chills wracked his body, and touching the Jew's forehead felt like pressing his palm to a freshly extinguished stovetop.

After trying unsuccessfully to use the scant resources available at Keidel Farm to bring down his lover's temperature, Franz finally conceded that he would need to go back to Headquarters and swipe some supplies.

"I'll be back soon," Franz promised, planting a hasty kiss on Amos' burning brow and running to the car. He was lucky that the checkpoints let him through even quicker this time; he declared that he had an emergency and they waved him on, wishing him luck, no doubt thinking that he was on some noble mission to help an imperiled SS comrade rather than rushing to steal Reich resources for a worthless Jew.

Franz was fortunate that he was the closest thing the

troop had to a medic. He didn't have a doctorate, of course, but a childhood of injuries far from a hospital had necessitated that he learn the basics of patching up wounds. He already had the key to their medicine closet without having to make a special request of Edmund Rahm, who seemed especially surly today. ("Don't mind him," chuckled Sigmund when he saw Franz swerve to avoid the fuming *Untersturmführer.* "My niece, you know, she's a lovely little trouble." Franz had never met Edmund Rahm's daughter, but given that she was the cause of fifty percent of Edmund Rahm's bad moods, he already didn't have a very good impression of the girl.)

He maneuvered past the Rahms and made it to the medicine closet, gathering some supplies and tossing them into a backpack.

"Private Keidel?"

Franz nearly dropped his bag. He made sure he was maintaining a neutral expression and then turned around. Dietrich was standing behind him, a half-smile decorating his young face.

"Heil Hitler," Franz said, slinging his backpack over his shoulder and shutting the medicine cabinet as casually as he could. Dietrich looked from the closet to the sack with a raised eyebrow.

"Aren't you off-duty today?" Dietrich asked. "Did, uh, did something happen?"

"Shoulder acting up again," Franz said in a brusque, almost aggressive tone. He didn't intend to be harsh, but he knew Dietrich still felt guilty about the incident with Black Fox 120. If anything would get him to drop it, it would be bringing up his injury.

"S-still...oh...I'm sorry about that," Dietrich mumbled, glancing nervously down at his jackboots. "I... sorry, I kind of just wanted to see if you...if you're...never mind...oh!"

Franz heard a soft rumbling noise by his ankles and looked down, unable to repress a smile when he saw Mausefalle the Second rubbing against his boots. Dietrich chuckled nervously and stooped down, gathering the troop's mascot into his arms. The tabby settled into his master's anxious embrace.

Amos was sick and needed help, and Franz really didn't have the time or the desire to chat with Dietrich, but something about the miserable way the young man cradled the cat reminded Franz too much of Amos when he was a boy. (Though of course if Amos had ever held Mausefalle the First like that, his face wouldn't be nearly as handsome as it was.)

"I'm in a rush," Franz said, softening his voice. "Walk with me to my car and tell me what you need to tell me."

Dietrich beamed like a boy that had been offered a trip to the candy shop. "Oh! Well, thank you! I was just… thinking very hard."

He trailed after Franz, chatting quickly as he pet the cat in his arms. "You know, the Führer is very great…I mean, of course you know that, haha! But I've admired him for so long because he's so *different*, nothing like other world leaders. Other world leaders only care about the people who can benefit them: the rich, the strong. But the Führer, he cares about all Germans. Children, the old, the sick, the oppressed Germans in the Sudetenland, and even German animals!"

Dietrich chuckled and held up Mausefalle the Second, who purred loudly.

"That, to me, that was very important!" Dietrich continued. "I've always loved animals. I grew up near a slaughterhouse, and I'd always hear the sounds of the pigs and cows being killed…it was awful. The Führer, he acknowledges that; he's even vegetarian, just like me! He's a truly empathetic man, the Führer, caring so much about the suffering of lesser beings. But…"

They walked by a portrait of the Führer. Adolf Hitler stood tall and bold, blue eyes fixed forward. Franz shivered, guilt clawing at his soul as he passed under his messiah's gaze.

"But I was thinking," Dietrich sighed, casting a gloomy look up at Hitler's visage, squeezing the cat tighter. "About what we did to that queer. N-not that I'm defending him, no! He's…homosexuals are obviously disgusting. But…I mean, pigs are disgusting too, yes? But the Führer wouldn't want to torture a pig."

Franz gripped the backpack tight and nodded once. A pig. He was lower than a swine.

"I just…" Dietrich stuttered. "I can't imagine the Führer would do *that* to that homosexual. I mean…it seemed just…needlessly cruel. We should be trying to help him, right? He's sick. We shouldn't just torture him; we should be trying to cure him. And if we can't cure him, then we should put him out of his misery, nice and quick and humane, like we did with the other sick people."

Franz's jaw tightened.

"But ripping out his nails just seemed…pointless. I don't think it fits the spirit of the Führer. It's…un-German."

Dietrich paused as they passed by the window to set Mausefalle the Second in his bed. The cat curled up and started snoozing. Franz picked up the pace, hoping that the younger man would become distracted by the cat. No such luck. Dietrich left the troop mascot and scurried to catch up, now walking at Franz's side.

"I mean…I agree with the war, of course," Dietrich mumbled, fiddling with a loose button on his uniform. "We have to defend ourselves against the enemy. But we're not just superior because we're stronger, or because we're more intelligent. We're superior because we're *ethical*. Jews and Bolsheviks, they torture animals, kill children, abuse the weak. That's why *they're* evil, that's why we *have* to fight them. For our children and our animals and our people...but if we act just like them, then..."

There was a heavy silence between the two SS men as they exited the building.

"I..." Dietrich said, and even though Franz refused to glance at his comrade, he knew that Dietrich must have been giving him a look of trust, a look of respect. "I was just thinking, because I saw your face in the interrogation, I think you...you may have been feeling the same way. I think...I think there must be a better way to fight this war. To fight it without losing our humanity. What...uh...what do you think?"

Franz was grateful to finally get to his car. He opened the door, tossed his backpack onto the passenger's seat, and gripped the car door handle so hard he was worried he might accidentally break it.

"Dietrich," he mumbled at last. "Have you...?"

He looked at the young SS man and hesitated. The thought that Amos wasn't actually *different*, the thought that Hitler was wrong...those treasonous thoughts returned with a fierce fury. He had always pushed them away, dismissed them as the imaginings of a sinner who, knowing of his fallen state, began to wonder if Satan was actually benevolent and God a tyrant.

But *if* those awful thoughts were true, then it was far too late for Franz, but Dietrich...

If Hitler was wrong, then Dietrich could still be a good person if he just stopped now before he went too far.

Perhaps it would be better that way. Even if they *weren't* wrong, Dietrich wouldn't be *evil* for simply giving up and walking away.

Still, encouraging an SS man to abandon the Cause would be a betrayal of his vow.

Then again, Franz had betrayed his vow enough already.

"Maybe…maybe you're just not cut out for the SS, have you ever thought of that?" Franz said. "Maybe you should consider going somewhere else, somewhere you'd be more…somewhere you wouldn't have to worry about this sort of thing."

He hoped that the younger man would thoughtfully ponder his words, perhaps mumble something in agreement. Of course, that was him being an optimist. Dietrich instead stared at him, sapphire eyes hardening, jaw tightening.

"You're saying I'm weak," growled the younger man.

Well, yes, thought Franz, but of course he couldn't say that. "No, I'm just saying that you might be able to better serve the Führer elsewhere, without having to…feel these things."

"I am not…I'm not a child, I'm just—I *am* tough, I belong in the SS!"

"I didn't say…ugh!" Franz pinched the bridge of his nose and shook his head. He simply didn't have time to argue about this. Amos needed him, and if he didn't leave now, the traffic would be impregnable.

"Look, I don't have time to play therapist, just…" Franz slid into the driver seat and fixed the scowling young SS man with a look of genuine concern. "Just do what you think is right."

The image of Dietrich's blazing sapphire eyes lingered in Franz's mind for some time as he fought traffic, but soon worry for Amos consumed his thoughts. By the time he got back to Keidel Farm, he had all but forgotten about his comrade.

"Amos!" Franz cried as he scurried into the house,

rushing to his lover's room with the backpack full of medicine. "Here, schatzi…oh, you're awake, good."

He entered the bedroom. As soon as he did, Amos sat bolt upright, gasping as though his head had been held underwater for five minutes.

For a moment, Franz was just grateful that Amos was able to sit up at all, but then he saw the absolute terror on his lover's face. Amos' eyes were wide, frenzied, like those of a rabbit that had been cornered by a fox. He gazed upon Franz with a cloudy sort of recognition, clutching his blanket with trembling hands.

"Amos?" Franz took a step forward and almost immediately regretted doing so. Amos let out a yelp like a puppy that had been smacked with a whip and threw himself back against the wall behind the head of the mattress, pressing his body against it as though he wanted nothing more than to somehow phase through the barrier and run as far from Franz as possible.

"N-not now," Amos stuttered, his voice hoarse and strained as he tried to get out a plea between bouts of rapid breathing. "Not now, please…"

Franz felt his stomach churn. "Amos," he said, trying to keep his tone as gentle as possible even as Amos' terrified eyes bored into him. It was a look Franz was used to: the look Jews gave him whenever he stumbled into their hiding place. It was the gaze of a child confronted by a monster.

"Amos, it's just me, you don't have to worry, I'm not going to hurt…"

He took another step forward. Amos wrapped one hand around his chest and covered his head with the other, as though he wanted to shield every part of his quaking body.

"D-don't…Kommandant Holzman…please, something else…just…please, no more…"

Franz felt as though his heart had been impaled with a burning needle. Hate, a familiar old friend, bombarded his soul. Hatred for the man whose name he now knew: Kommandant Holzman, the monster that had hurt his Amos.

But then...then he realized with a woozy sensation that Amos thought *he* was the same monster. He knew the creature's name now, but he didn't know what he looked like. Perhaps Amos was simply so sick that he was seeing a complete stranger, but the thought that he resembled Holzman enough that Amos' illness-addled mind would even begin to connect the two of them...

Franz looked down at himself, at his SS uniform, at his Reich decorations, at the swastika on his arm, and realized that even if he and Kommandant Holzman looked completely different, their shared uniform might have made them seem identical. In the shadows, one SS man looked just like any other. Nothing more than a Jew's nightmare given form.

Recognizing this made the uniform feel heavy. Hoping that taking it off would render him human again, Franz started to unbutton his coat.

This was the wrong course of action. Amos saw the SS man begin to disrobe and his pleadings became incomprehensibly desperate. Sobs wracked his small body, and the sound of his wailing was easily the worst noise Franz had ever heard in his life. *"Pleasepleasepleasdon't youpromisedpleasedon'tpleaseplease!"*

"I...I'm sorry!" Franz cried, holding up his hands as though to surrender, leaving his damned uniform half undone. "I'm sorry, Amos..."

Amos' crying might have made Franz break down himself, but he couldn't afford to. He needed to help him, somehow.

An idea struck and he hastily retreated from the room,

snatching a book off the nightstand in the living room. He returned to find that his temporary absence hadn't alleviated Amos' terror. The Jew had stopped pleading and instead just sat, shielding himself and sobbing so loudly that Franz was worried he might alert the neighbors despite the thick walls and distance.

"All right, it's all right, I'm not coming near...here..." Franz crept along the wall of the bedroom, keeping as far from Amos as possible before sliding down and sitting on the floor. He held up the book he had retrieved: Amos' copy of *White Fang*, which by now they had read together so many times that Franz likely could have recited it by memory.

He saw Amos peek past his arms. The Jew probably couldn't even see through the tears streaming from his turquoise eyes, but at the very least he must have recognized that Franz's behavior would have been completely out of character for Kommandant Holzman.

Franz found the most dog-eared section of the book, Amos' favorite part. The chapter where the wild wolf-dog became tame. Inhaling deeply, he forced his tone to become gentle and calming as he read aloud:

"*'Having learned to snuggle, White Fang was guilty of it often. It was the final word. He could not go beyond it. The one thing of which he had always been particularly jealous was his head. He had always disliked to have it touched. It was the Wild in him, the fear of hurt and of the trap, that had given rise to panicky impulses to avoid contact...'*"

As he read, Franz continuously looked up, watching with relief as Amos lowered his defenses bit by bit. The Jew's arms fell limp to his sides, his tense shoulders became slack, and the terror in his eyes became blurry confusion.

"*'...his snuggling was a deliberate act of putting himself into a position of hopeless helplessness. It was an expression of perfect confidence, of absolute self-surrender..."'*

"Hahnchen..." Amos' voice was soft and wary. Franz looked up and sighed happily when he discovered that his lover had curled up on his side. Fear had left Amos' eyes, replaced with exhausted affection. Franz desperately wanted to crawl towards him and kiss him, embrace him, comfort him, but he feared that doing so would only frighten the Jew once more.

"Right here, schatzi," he assured him. "You don't have to worry. Do you want me to read some more?"

Amos let out a small affirmative noise, his eyes slowly closing as Franz continued to read. The SS man didn't dare move until he was certain that he had successfully lulled his lover to sleep. Sighing with relief, he shut the book and crawled to Amos, picking him up and tucking him back in. He retrieved his backpack, treated Amos as well as he could without waking him and then, exhausted, sat at his side, gently stroking the Jew's cheek with the back of his hand.

"You didn't even tell me half of what that monster did to you. You poor thing," Franz whispered. "Holzman...as soon as I get the chance, I promise you..."

Even in his sleep, it seemed that Amos heard the name of his tormenter. He whimpered softly. Franz heaved an exhausted sigh and kissed Amos' brow.

"Nobody's going to hurt you again," he vowed, but a voice, alien and yet frighteningly familiar, whispered from the depths of his mind.

You hurt him.

He felt his heart freeze.

You hurt him just by being here. He was terrified of you.

Franz looked down at his wrinkled, half-unbuttoned SS uniform.

He should be terrified of you.

Slowly, he righted his uniform. Buttoned up the tunic.

What's the difference between you and Holzman, really? Sure, he raped him, but he didn't even think he was a real person.

Straightened out his swastika armband.

He isn't a person, right?

It's different, he tried to argue in his mind, but the new voice all but chortled at this.

To *you* he's different. And if Dietrich fell madly in love with that queer you tortured or Black Fox 120, would *that* be different too? You would *never* accept that. Nobody would. Hypocrite. If Holzman's a monster, then you're a monster too.

Franz hissed and shook his head. *That's stupid, that's wrong, I am not a monster. I would never do something like **that** to anyone...*

Oh. So you wouldn't *rape* a Jew, you'd just kill them. How noble. How ethical. Amos only loves you because he thinks *you're* different. He thinks he can tame you like that wolf-dog.

Franz's eyes flitted to *White Fang.*

But he can't. You're already feral. The voice became softer, almost pained.

That look he gave you...if he saw what you did every day, if he knew that you can't be fixed...you're lying to him every time you come here and pretend to be good.

Franz felt ill.

If you love him at all, you should let him go. Don't pretend like you can't figure something out. There's a high-ranked Black Fox at the base. If you really love him, you should let him go before you hurt him again.

And Franz shook his head and forced the soft voice to silence itself. But as he stared at Amos' tranquil, tear-stained face and pictured the terrified look the Jew had given him, he felt a familiar ripping sensation claw at his soul.

CHAPTER TEN

Amos recovered, and the gentle voice didn't resurface. For some time, Franz was only reminded of the awful incident when he himself had nightmares. Nightmares of Amos looking at him in terror, nightmares of hurting him, nightmares of being Kommandant Holzman.

The nightmares made an already fraught sleeping schedule almost unfeasible, which meant that he began to make more mistakes at work. Most of them were forgivable: a slip of the hand here, a sloppy take-down there, one occasion where he accidentally hit a fatal artery on a prisoner Sigmund had hoped to keep alive. Mistakes that were probably keeping him from becoming a Sergeant. Fortunately, the Rahms were too focused on Dietrich to even notice his slip-ups half the time.

The younger SS man had evidently taken Franz's suggestion as a challenge and was absolutely determined to prove that he belonged in the SS. He volunteered for guard duty to the point where his feet were probably aching. He was the first to kick down doors, the first to charge into a potential Black Fox lair, the first to grab a

Jew by the arm and wrench them out of their hiding place, the first to strike them with a merciless fury that seemed alien to his nature.

Sigmund was talking about promoting him. Even Edmund was impressed with his improvement.

But something about watching the light in Dietrich's youthful sapphire eyes turn into a frosty emptiness that would have made Reinhard Heydrich proud was deeply disturbing to Franz. Distinctly, he wondered if *his* eyes had looked like that. He wondered if that was why Amos hadn't even recognized him when they'd first reunited in Winkler's barn.

Either way, Franz tried his best not to think about it. He had too much to ponder anyway. Mueller had started whispering that they were likely going to be transferred soon. If that happened, it would happen quickly. Franz wouldn't have much time, and so his mind was abuzz as he tried to plot out what he would do if it became absolutely necessary to move Amos. It would all depend on where they were transferred, of course. If they were lucky, he could still maintain their semi-comfortable status quo.

Of course, the question of whether or not he *should* was beginning to bother him.

For a while, however, he was able to put those thoughts aside. Dietrich began doing most of his work for him. For some time, Franz didn't even lay a finger on a prisoner, and his soul began to feel strangely light. Hugging Amos felt even better knowing that his hands were temporarily clean. Sure, he was stressed and getting even less sleep than usual thanks to the nightmares, but things were *decent.*

Of course, *decent* couldn't last long.

And one night, he was sent on a mission with Edmund Rahm and Dietrich. Out to an abandoned house that had evidently been the source of strange noises. High-pitched noises.

They arrived on the property just as the sun was setting and the sky was splashed crimson. Edmund immediately spotted a shed on the far corner of the property, shadowed and strangely well-kept.

"One of you go investigate that shed," Edmund commanded in a hiss. "The other stays with me. We go into the house together."

"I'll go check out the shed," Dietrich volunteered, and Franz bit back a sigh of relief. If there was a Jew or a Black Fox, they were likely in the shed. He would prefer it if he didn't have to deal with a weight on his soul tonight. He desperately wanted to get this over with, get back to Amos and hold him with relatively clean hands.

"Good," Edmund grunted, gesturing for Dietrich to go. "Then you're with me, Keidel."

"Yes, sir."

While Dietrich snuck towards his target, Franz and Edmund drew their guns and crept close to the house's cellar door. They stood on either side of the hatch. Franz grabbed the handle and glanced at his superior, waiting for the command.

"One...two..."

No three. Edmund simply pointed at the door. Franz turned the handle, but he had barely lifted the hatch when it flew open, smacking him in the face and sending him careening into a patch of moist moss.

"Unk! Keidel!" An exclamation from Edmund made Franz's dizziness dissipate. He looked up just in time to see a red-haired man—a Jew if the Yiddish curses that flew from his mouth were any indication—grab Edmund's arm. The Jew and the *Untersturmführer* fought for the gun.

The Jewish man screamed something in Yiddish, and the Judaic tongue was close enough to German that Franz was able to pick out one word: "Run!"

Franz started to scramble to his feet, one hand flying

to his gun, ready to open fire on the battalion of Black Foxes that was sure to swarm him.

But no soldiers emerged from the basement. Only one creature popped out and started sprinting towards the thicket: a little girl with a curly bob of red hair, dressed in a scrappy red dress. Not a day older than nine, tears streaming down her face as she briefly met Franz's gaze. The look she gave him was too much like the expression Amos had offered when he'd thought Franz was Kommandant Holzman.

Bang! A gunshot rang out and Franz looked towards Edmund. The *Untersturmführer* had successfully wrestled his gun from the Jew and fired at the fugitive's chest. The Jewish man crumpled to the dirt, twitching once before going still. The Jewish girl was wise enough not to look back. She ran, gasping and sobbing as she tried to make it to the safety of the forest.

Edmund huffed, righted his uniform, and then looked up at the fleeing Jewish child. His eyes widened a fraction and he knelt down, searching the Jew he had just shot, turning his back on the retreating girl.

"Keidel, shoot her!"

In the days that followed, Franz would bitterly wonder why Edmund hadn't just shot her himself. But right then, he asked no questions. He had been given an order. A **command.** His SS training went to work as he stood, pulled out his gun, and aimed at the retreating figure.

What do you think of kids? Amos' voice echoed in his ears. His hand trembled. The girl looked back, her blue eyes wide and human.

Fantasies invaded his mind. Amos laughing as the troop of orphans he'd collected greeted a returning Franz with happy shrieks. Little feet running across the floor of a sanctuary, tiny hands fighting to embrace him first.

"Keidel!"

His finger was on the trigger. He'd never shot a child before.

"KEIDEL!"

It was the right thing to do. Shooting her, it would be the right thing to do. She was a Jew. Letting her live would put German children in danger. She would grow and come back and avenge herself upon the German people.

"KEIDEL, SHOOT NOW!"

In his mind, Franz told Amos what he had done and his beloved looked at him, not with hate, but with agony. He wouldn't hate Franz; he would hate himself for not being able to save him.

"I...I can't..." Franz gasped, lowering his gun. Edmund snarled.

"Useless! Dietrich, **fire**!"

Dietrich! Franz had almost completely forgotten that his comrade was present. The Jewish child was almost at the forest line, but Dietrich, standing in front of the empty shed, was close to her, close enough to have a clear shot.

The younger SS man reacted to Edmund's command as though the *Untersturmführer's* will was his own. Suddenly, like a puppet whose strings had been tugged, he pulled out his gun and aimed at the fleeing child.

A memory struck Franz. A promise he had made to himself the day he'd found Amos in Winkler's barn. A promise that he would kill any child they found so that Dietrich wouldn't have to.

He raised up his gun, aimed, pressed his finger to the trigger.

BANG!

Too late. Dietrich shot first. The girl crumpled, blood pooling beneath her little frame, staining the mossy ground.

The next few hours after that were a blur. He would remember Edmund's garbled critique of his weakness. He would remember watching Edmund congratulate Dietrich, even patting the shoulder of the quaking SS man. He would remember watching the light in Dietrich's eyes fade into a cold void as the boy forced his heart to become iron. He would remember the sickening sensation of shame filling him. Shame because he hadn't saved Dietrich. Shame because he had almost shot a child. He would remember getting in his car after he was dismissed and trying not to cry. He would remember failing that task.

A part of him wanted to stay away from Amos, for he knew that what they had needed to end. He couldn't tell him what he had almost done. He couldn't tell him what had happened. But even if Amos never found out, Franz knew, and that was already too much.

But then, the daze cleared, and he found himself standing in the threshold of the farmhouse. Amos was running to greet him, smiling. When he saw Franz's horrified countenance and tear-stained cheeks, the Jew's smile morphed into an expression of concern.

"Hahnchen…"

He started to reach for him, to hug him, to comfort him. Franz leapt back, shaking his head.

"Don't," he begged, and he was surprised by the sound of his own voice. He sounded like an eight-year-old boy again, a boy begging his friend not to try and save him.

Amos winced and clutched the end of his turquoise scarf. He was quiet for a moment, chewing on his tongue as he tried to find the words. Finally, he timidly asked, "Did something happen? You can tell me. I promise I won't hate you, whatever it is."

Franz knew Amos was telling the truth, and that made it worse.

"Amos…" He leaned against the wall, trying not to look at his lover, staring down at his dirty uniform, at the grime-stained medals, at the gun holstered on the belt emblazoned with the SS motto: *My Honor is My Loyalty!*

He let out a noise that was half a chuckle, half a sob. "Amos...you really want to know why I joined the SS?"

Slowly, Amos nodded. "If you want to tell me."

It didn't matter what Franz wanted. He wondered if it had ever mattered. Taking in a shuddering breath, he glanced at the empty space in the living room where his father's cozy chair had once stood.

"Do you know why my father hated me?" he asked, and Amos fidgeted with the end of his scarf.

"I...wondered."

"I killed my mother. That's why."

"When you were born? Oh, Franz..."

"No." He bit his lip hard enough to break skin. "No. Birth was fine. No problems. Healthy baby. Healthy mom. But...something strange happened after I was born. I don't remember her at all, but Papa used to say she was a living flame. Bright and happy all the time. But when I was born, something changed and that flame...died. From the moment she held me, she just looked down at me and didn't...feel anything. She hated me...she *hated* me."

"Oh..." Amos reached out once more, and again Franz pulled away.

"I don't know why. She was miserable. Like my existence broke her."

"Franz..."

"She killed herself when I was two. Jumped off the roof. She hated me so much she killed herself."

"You can't blame yourself...and if your father blamed you..."

"He used to say I stole her soul. He used to call me a little monster. A demon. A murderer."

He was right.

"Franz, please, you know he was wrong." Amos

squeezed his hand. "You're not a monster. You're not responsible for what happened to your mother. And whatever you've done in the SS, I know you didn't mean...I *know* you're a good person, you've just been brainwashed..."

He's wrong.

"Father hated Hitler," Franz finally said. "Used to call him a stupid little corporal. Of course, I thought that if a man like my father hated Hitler, that meant Hitler must be truly great. Everything's like that, isn't it? Evil or good. One or the other."

"Franz...I..."

"Father was bad, so Hitler was good. I'd listen to his speeches when the old man fell asleep. And I'd listen, and he'd talk, and sometimes he'd talk about Jews, and that was all well because I didn't...I didn't even think I knew one. I wonder what I would have done if you'd told me earlier..."

"I...kind of wish I had, but...to be honest, everyone hated Jews back then, even before Hitler. I was sort of worried you might...hate me. That you wouldn't want to be my friend anymore. But I was wrong!"

"Amos...I just..." Franz sucked in a sharp breath and felt like his chest was going to explode. "He...Hitler...he used to say that Germans were *worth* something. Germans were pure and strong and good. *All* Germans. Even me. Sometimes it felt like he was speaking right to me, like he was my real father. I remember I used to *wish* he was my real father. You and Hitler, you both kept *me* from jumping off the roof when I was a kid."

"Franz..."

"I couldn't do anything for you, but I realized one day that I could do something for Hitler. So I ran. And I served the National Socialists. Cleaned their toilets, delivered their messages, did everything they wanted. Clawed my way up....because I was grateful, because I believed everything Hitler said, because I *wanted* to believe it so badly. But if he was wrong…"

"Hahnchen…"

"You want...you *need* me to choose between you and him, and I can't. I *can't*, Amos. If he's wrong, then Father was right. He was so right about me…"

"No, no, no, no, no, that is *not* what I'm saying, Franz! Please, listen!" Amos yelped, closing the chasm between them and forcing his lover into an embrace. "It's not black and white! You're a good person no matter what Hitler or your father or the Black Foxes say! No matter what! I love you no matter what!"

"I know, Amos, I know," Franz said, hesitantly returning the embrace even though he knew it was wrong. "I love you too. No matter what. That's the problem."

That's why you have to leave.

CHAPTER ELEVEN

"Leave?! No!"

"Amos…."

"I won't leave! I don't want to leave, I…"

"Amos, I just got word today. We can't put this off anymore."

"Word…?"

"My troop is being transferred to some shithole called Brennenbach. I can't take care of you anymore."

"F-Franz…"

"It's better this way, Amos."

No more Amos. No more questions. No more moments of happiness stolen by reality. No more waves of self-hatred. He could cover his heart in ice again.

"F-Franz…if this is your way of breaking up…"

"Amos…" He cupped his lover's face in his hands. "You have no idea how much I wish it didn't have to be like this. I wish we could live somewhere else, I wish we were different people, I wish we could just be *us*. But reality is reality. I love you and I want you to be safe. I want you to be happy, even if it means being happy without me."

"The war will end."

"Amos…"

"I'll do whatever you tell me to, but don't tell me not to wait for you. The war will end, and I'll find you."

"Schatzi…"

"*I'll find you.* We'll be together if I have to tear the world in two."

His turquoise eyes flashed with the intensity of an archangel preparing to challenge God, and Franz knew that while the world would try its best to keep Amos from fulfilling that vow, it was in for one Hell of a battle.

"Just be happy, please, no matter what," Franz begged. "Adopt your orphans and be happy and be safe."

Amos chuckled. "I'll come back, find you, drag you off to our new home in the middle of nowhere, and you'll be buried in orphans. All right…so what's the plan?"

THE PLAN: Black Fox 120, the Black Fox that had stabbed Franz's shoulder, was still locked in one of the prison cells at HQ. As a relatively high-ranked member of the resistance group, there was no doubt that he would know of a way to smuggle Amos to safety.

The Problem: Reinhard Heydrich.

Really, it was just like Heydrich to butt in at the worst possible moment. Heydrich was the architect of the Final Solution, the chief of a multitude of vitally genocidal departments: the SD, the RSHA, the Gestapo. Sigmund Rahm and his men were at Heydrich's beck and call, and none of them were happy about that. Stick any SS man in a room with Joseph Stalin, Reinhard Heydrich, and a gun with one bullet, and while that SS man would have probably ended up shooting Stalin, it would have only been after several minutes of careful deliberation.

Sigmund in particular had always hated Heydrich. When the older Rahm brother burst into the office one day, cursing the name of the so-called Blonde Beast, Franz knew they were in for a headache. It was easy enough to get advanced notice of Heydrich's meddling since Sigmund was only too eager to vent.

"Asshole's got some pet project going on in the Protectorate. Something about the Black Foxes, some plan to make himself the future Führer. Hell if I know the specifics, but he wants *all* the Black Foxes that *we* caught! He's sending some of his men to collect 'em on Sunday."

Sunday. Instead of having a month to get Amos to safety, Franz now had less than a week. He pictured that scenario involving Stalin, Heydrich, and one bullet, and decided he would resolve such a dilemma by shooting Stalin in the head and then beating Heydrich to death with the gun. A bullet would be too good for the Butcher of Prague if Amos got hurt because of him.

Thankfully, Sigmund's tantrum managed to draw the attention of Franz's comrades. While Major Rahm screeched about Billy-Goat Heydrich sticking his big Jew nose into everything, Franz slipped into the prison block and found Black Fox 120's cell.

"Psst!" he hissed, kneeling by the bars and scowling at the crumpled figure inside. Black Fox 120 looked better now than he had when he was a fresh addition to the prison. He had been unbreakable as of yet, refusing to say a word about his organization. His recalcitrance had been aggravating for Franz at first, but now it was a good sign. The man was loyal to his virtues, loyal and willing to endure horrific torture for the sake of helpless Jews like Amos.

Thankfully, Sigmund had decided that killing Black

Fox 120 would be a waste of energy. It was better to let him get better and then try some new interrogation methods. He was starving now, but able. No broken limbs, minimal wounds. He could make it. He could save Amos.

The Black Fox regarded him with a venomous scowl. 120 spat at Franz, hissing a curse in Russian.

Sighing, Franz wiped the spittle off his cheek. "I'm not here to interrogate you, and I don't have much time. Listen to me: I want to set you free. This isn't a trap, this isn't a trick. I'll set you free, but you have to save someone for me."

The Black Fox lifted an unkempt brow, glancing nervously at the slightly open door that separated the prison from the office.

"I know you understand me, please," Franz whispered. "Please, I know how this looks, I know I'm a hypocrite, but I have a Jew. He needs help, he's hiding in a farmhouse all by himself. I don't care what it takes, I need you to save him. I have a plan to get you out, but I need you to promise me you'll save him."

120's striking blue eyes narrowed. Franz felt his heart shudder as, unbidden, the memory of looking into identical eyes struck. His hand burned.

The SS man clasped his hands in front of his chest, a small sob wracking his body.

"Please, *please*, I don't know what else to do," Franz begged. "I'll let you kill me if that's what it takes, but you *have* to save him..."

"This Jew..." The Black Fox spoke in German for the first time since he had been captured. His accent was thick, but his linguistic skill was still admirable. "What is he to you?"

Franz swallowed. There was a chance even this relatively liberal Black Fox wouldn't be willing to help a queer.

"He's my childhood best friend," said Franz, not technically lying. "I owe him my life. I need to save him, whatever the cost."

"Whatever your plan is…if you live through it, your comrades will be suspicious," the Black Fox said.

"Then kill me, it's fine! As long as you save him, I don't care if I die!"

The Black Fox's eyes shimmered thoughtfully. He touched his heart, laying his hand over a wound he'd had before Rahm's troop captured him. After an agonizing moment of contemplation, 120 grunted and gave a small nod.

"Where is he now?" the Black Fox asked.

"You promise…"

"I've kept my mouth shut this long, Nazi. I don't particularly care about your feelings, but I'm not going to get a Jew hurt just to spite you. Tell me where he is and tell me this plan."

"F-Friday?!" Amos' voice cracked.

"Friday night. It's the only time we can move."

"Why?"

"Black Fox One-Twenty is locked up tight, and the base is crawling with my comrades during the day. A daytime escape is completely unfeasible, but at night, there are only ever two guards. Friday night is my shift, so we're going to make it look like he broke out. He'll pretend to be sick, I'll go in to check on him, then he'll 'steal my knife'…"

And kill me if he has to; if he feels that it's necessary.

Franz, of course, wasn't going to tell Amos about that optional step in the plan.

"Then he'll steal my uniform, my car, and he'll come to the farmhouse. He said he'll knock on the door seven times and when you answer, he'll ask if you're ready to go see Papa. You'll answer, 'Yes, but I don't have a gift to bring him.' Got it? 'Yes, but I have no gift.' You must say that, so he knows you're the pick-up."

"Yes, but I have no gift…" muttered Amos thrice, searing the code phrase into his brain before nodding. "Okay, I think I've got it. W-wait, you said there are always *two* SS men on duty at night."

Franz clenched his teeth together. "Yes."

"So…what will happen to the other SS man? Won't he try to stop Black Fox One-Twenty?"

Franz let out a shuddering breath. "Mueller is going to be on duty with me. I'll have to eliminate him before I release Black Fox One-Twenty."

Mueller was a loyal SS man, as dirty as any, a man who would never hesitate to put a bullet in a Jewish child's brain. Sure, Franz had always considered him something of an acquaintance, but he had vowed long ago that he would kill any of his comrades for Amos. If he had to kill one, he was grateful it was Mueller. He only wished he could stab Edmund Rahm instead.

"Franz…" Amos suddenly threw himself forward, wrapping his arms around Franz's waist, and any lingering hesitation the SS officer might have felt at the thought of murdering his comrade vanished.

"It's all right," Franz whispered in his lover's ear, embracing him almost too tightly. "Don't worry about it."

"I'm sorry you have to hurt your friend. I'm sorry…" Amos sounded so genuinely upset. Upset! At an SS man killing another Nazi! It was almost funny. Of course, Amos didn't care one bit about Mueller, but he cared so much about Franz, about how much this would hurt Franz…

"It's not your fault, don't worry about it. You're so good," Franz mumbled, heart swelling with fondness for the Jewish man. He buried his face in the soft fabric of the turquoise scarf.

"You're worth it," Franz said. "Okay? You're worth it. Don't feel bad."

"All right. Damn. I wish…I thought we'd have more time together."

"Let's…just enjoy what we have," Franz said, and Amos nodded, planting a determined kiss on Franz's cheek.

"I'T'S TIME."

Franz almost didn't want to say goodbye. He could tell from Amos' eyes that he didn't either, but the Jew still insisted on smiling. Smiling the way he had before, when he'd fractured the shield of ice Franz had formed around his heart.

"This isn't goodbye," Amos declared, looping his arms around Franz's neck, his gentle voice resolute. "We'll see each other again. I promise."

Franz didn't want to argue. It was pointless, and he didn't want to extinguish the hope in Amos' eyes. He just wanted to hold him and kiss him one last time. Tonight, he would either die for him or he would have to forget him. Either way, he would never see him again.

"I love you," Franz whispered, kissing Amos deeply. Breaking away from him felt like ripping off his own arm, but he did so.

"I love you…and I *will* find you again. I love you no matter what!" Amos announced.

"No matter what…" Franz whispered, smiling once more at his love before turning away and practically running to his car.

The trip to SS HQ felt like it took days. He lingered in the vehicle for a moment when he parked, gripping the steering wheel and fighting to control his hammering heart. This walk from the car to the dreary building could be his last. His last time outside. These hours were likely his last.

For Amos, he reminded himself, and he exited the car, enjoying the drizzle of rain that caressed him as he slowly trudged towards HQ. It felt good. Refreshing. And it would provide good cover for Black Fox 120.

He entered the building.

"Rainy outside, hm?"

His heart almost stopped.

"Dietrich…" he muttered. The younger SS man was sitting behind his desk, cleaning his gun.

"What are you doing here?" Franz asked, struggling to maintain a casual tone. "I thought Mueller was on duty tonight."

"He wanted off, and I offered to cover for him," Dietrich said. "Didn't feel like sitting around. You sound sort of disappointed. I can promise you I won't be a burden."

Dietrich looked up, the edge of his lip twitching as he offered an almost agonizing impersonation of a smile. Franz felt bile rise in his throat and silently cursed Mueller for making such a request of Dietrich. Of all the SS men in his troop, Dietrich, the man he had failed so thoroughly, was the one he wanted to kill the least.

For Amos, he reminded himself again. "I know you won't be a burden, I'm just surprised."

"Hm…" Dietrich barely seemed to hear his comrade. He was scrubbing the Luger with a strangely hollow expression.

"I…uh…" Franz almost muttered that the gun was clean already, almost asked Dietrich why he was scrubbing it, but he knew why and he didn't want to make Dietrich's last moments more unpleasant than necessary.

"I'm...going to check on the prisoners," Franz announced. Dietrich nodded.

Franz poked his head into the prison corridor, his eyes flitting to Black Fox 120's cell. The Black Fox was leaning against the rusted bars. Their gazes met for one moment before Franz held up a finger, a gesture to wait until he...

He exhaled. *Dietrich....*

Having confirmed that Black Fox 120 was ready to go, Franz slowly approached Dietrich. He drew his knife from its sheath and held it behind his back, creeping close. A part of him wanted to just strike, knowing that speaking to the younger man would only make this harder.

But as he drew close, he noticed that Dietrich looked absolutely awful. His eyes were weighed down by heavy bags, his skin seemed unusually pale, and his eyes were lightless. The young man's hands trembled as he continuously cleaned the same spot on his gun over and over, as though he was trying to self-soothe but without...

Franz glanced around the darkened office and realized that Dietrich was cleaning his gun instead of petting Mausefalle the Second. In fact, all the trappings of their so-called mascot were gone. His toys were no longer littering the floor, his food and water bowl were no longer set up beside Dietrich's desk, even his little bed was gone.

"Hey...where's Mausefalle?" Franz asked. Dietrich's jaw tightened.

"The cat?" he said, and Franz nodded. Dietrich exhaled slowly through his nostrils and scrubbed his gun even more aggressively.

"I gave him away," Dietrich said. "To my landlady. It's better. She has lots of cats."

"Oh...I'm sure he's happy, but..." Franz muttered, tightening his grip on the blade still hidden behind his back. "I thought he was our mascot."

Dietrich's hollow eyes came to life for a brief moment,

but not with the youthful twinkle they had once possessed. It was a blazing flash that reminded him of Sigmund Rahm.

"Don't be a child," Dietrich said, his tone harsh, biting. "We're an SS troop. We have *important* work to do."

He put brutal emphasis on the word "important." Franz felt his heart plummet to the bottom of his chest. He had felt like a worthless waste of air in the past, but never more so than he did right then. Suddenly, his impending death didn't seem too terrible. Not compared to what he was about to do to Dietrich. Not compared to what he'd already done.

Then again, maybe this was mercy.

"Dietrich...are you okay?" It almost felt like a laughable query to offer a man he was about to kill, but Franz asked anyway. He almost shivered when Dietrich responded with a mirthless chuckle.

"You know...my name's not Dietrich," the younger man said, finally setting down his gun and leaning back in his seat, staring at the barrel of the weapon he had used to end a child's life. "That's my last name. Franz, do you even know my first name?"

"Oh...uh...no, not really...sorry," Franz confessed. Really, except for the Rahm brothers whose first names he knew out of necessity, he didn't know *any* of his comrades' first names. They all called one another by rank, by surname, by fond insults. Even hearing his own first name fall from Dietrich's lips was strange, strange and almost painful.

"Hm...we've all worked together for so long," Dietrich muttered, smirking bitterly. "We're supposed to be brothers, but I don't know. I sometimes feel like we're all actually strangers. Like we don't know each other, like we don't even want to…"

His smirk wilted away. "My first name's Hans. Nothing special."

"Hans," repeated Franz. The name tasted sour.

Hans Dietrich smiled. "Huh...you know, I think it's been years since I've heard my own name. Except when we arrest Jews, you know. Or kill them. Lots of Hanses. It's always a little weird, you know. 'Don't hurt Hans, Hans please, Hans, Hans, Hans.' And it always feels like they're talking to me or about me, but...that's silly."

"I understand how you feel," Franz whispered. "There are a lot of Jews named Franz."

"You know, I have a little sister, too..." Dietrich mumbled. "Well, I *had* one. She died when we were kids."

"I..."

"Measles. Typical. Nothing special. Hm..."

Hans Dietrich gingerly ran his fingers over the shimmering gun before him. "Wonder what she'd think of her big brother. You think she'd be proud?"

Franz tried desperately to force an icy shield around his heart. "I don't know," he whispered, which was the only thing he could say without lying.

"I don't either," Dietrich confessed, and for a moment it seemed he might break. His voice cracked, his hands trembled, but then he wrapped the protective and comforting mantle of a merciless SS man around his soul.

"It doesn't matter," Dietrich declared, and if he didn't actually believe that, he sounded like he did. "It doesn't matter what she'd think. We've got a job to do."

"Hans..." Franz steeled himself, inhaling deeply. "I'm sorry."

Hans Dietrich didn't even get to cry out. There was a sickening gurgle and a noise that reminded Franz of the sound a pig made when gutted. The blade went right through Dietrich's neck.

One sob escaped Franz's throat as his knees buckled

and he knelt beside his comrade's body, retching and gasping and muttering garbled apologies to the dead SS man. If he wasn't a murderer because of what he had done to the Jews, he was a murderer now. Just like Father always said.

*Amos, Amos, Amos...*he thought of his love and a surge of strength let him rise to his feet and pull his blade from the SS man's corpse. He stabbed the slumped-over body a few more times for the sake of the ruse before scurrying into the prison. He opened the cell door and dropped his bloody blade at the Black Fox's feet.

"Strip," the Black Fox commanded, grabbing the blade and the keys. "Your Jew's ready for extraction?"

"Y-Yes," Franz gasped, letting tears flow freely as he took off his SS tunic and handed it to the Black Fox. Shedding the uniform he had once adored felt strangely good. Like removing a robe made of fire.

The Black Fox's magnetic blue eyes stared unblinkingly at the softly sobbing SS man and he gently queried, "Are you ready?"

"Yes." No pause. He was eager to feel nothing.

The Black Fox put on his uniform. He was unshaved and dark-haired, but he could pass for an SS man as long as nobody looked too closely or heard him speak with a Russian accent. He could make it.

"Don't tell him," Franz begged, slipping into the cell and staring at the blade in the Black Fox's hand, his gut writhing. A part of him, the animalistic part that just wanted to survive, objected to this foolishness, but the rest of his soul braced itself for oblivion. "Don't tell him what you did, okay? Don't tell him."

"I won't," the Black Fox promised. "Any...any last requests? I'll try not to, but I have to make it convincing or they'll kill you even if I don't, and then you'd have to worry about your family and..."

138

"I don't have anyone except the Jew," Franz said. "Don't worry. It doesn't matter. Just do what you have to do."

The Black Fox nodded. Franz shut his eyes.

Pain! Pain! Pain! Instinct made him lash out once or twice, but it didn't matter. The Black Fox was armed, and he was as helpless as he had been when he was a little boy facing his father. He felt his life drain from him as agony made him collapse, but he heard the Black Fox's footsteps. Heard him release a few of the other able Black Foxes. Heard him raid the office and escape. Heard him promise to save the Jew.

The Jew. Amos.

Thinking of him was almost as painful as the wounds, but he would be safe. That made all of this worth it.

He thought of Amos until he could think no longer, and darkness overtook him.

CHAPTER TWELVE

Franz was deeply upset when he awoke a few weeks later. Not in Hell, but in a hospital. The Black Fox hadn't killed him. *Idiot.*

He looked to his bedside and found it covered in gifts. Bouquets, little flags, get-well soon cards covered in swastikas and SS runes. One card that sat in front of every other offering bore the distinctive signature of Heinrich Himmler, head of the SS.

So they didn't know he was a traitor. *Good.*

Amos…

His heart started hammering. He barely heard the nurse greet him sweetly and announce that she would inform Sigmund Rahm that he was awake.

The wait was as agonizing as his injuries, but he sat, brimming with anxiety, until Sigmund Rahm arrived with a smile.

"There's our boy!" the Major said, clapping the injured SS man on the shoulder. "We've been worried about you!"

"What happened?" Franz asked.

"Frankly, I was going to ask you the same thing. We all

assumed the Black Fox somehow overpowered you, grabbed your dagger. We found you half-dead in the cell when we came into the office. Thought you *were* dead, but you hung in there. Black Fox missed the vital shit by millimeters."

"Black Fox...grabbed me...stabbed me..." Franz mumbled, and though he was truly a bit dazed, he could just barely remember the cover story he and Black Fox 120 had come up with.

"Easy, son, I imagine it's not a pleasant memory, being stabbed eleven times," Sigmund said, patting the SS Private's bandaged shoulder. "You don't remember anything specific?"

"Not...really. Head fuzzy."

"Understandable. We're just glad you made it. The whole affair was awful. We lost the Black Foxes and...well, I don't mean to upset you..."

"Dietrich," Franz muttered, trying to make fright over-power the sorrow in his tone, trying to pretend that he didn't know what had become of his comrade.

"He got caught by surprise, poor lad. He was already exhausted. Should have given him time off...shouldn't have let him take Mueller's shift. He died a proper SS man. Wish you had been awake for the funeral. Himmler didn't show himself, but he sent a bouquet. His parents are very proud of their boy..."

Sigmund let out a heavy sigh and Franz felt ill seeing the guilt in his commander's eyes. The Major's gaze flitted to the pile of cards and flowers on Franz's bedstand, glazing over a bit as he no doubt recalled his young under-ling's funeral.

"The Black Foxes," Franz said, forcing his guilt to recede and remembering his lover. "Did you catch them? Do you have any leads?"

It was hard to hide his relief when Sigmund let out a

frustrated sigh. "Nothing yet. Heydrich's about to flay my hide for this. It's a disaster, and right before we were about to move. I'm lucky they're desperate to fill that Kommandant position and everyone's too busy talking about Viktor Naden to focus on this fuck-up, but...enough! Don't you worry about it. We'll find them, we'll get them back for what they did to you and Dietrich."

Franz nodded, biting back a reassured exhale. It had been weeks, and they hadn't been caught. *Then Amos is safe...assuming they kept their word and got him.*

The thought that they *hadn't* immediately wormed its way into his brain and filled him with a fresh bout of agitation. "How long until I can get back to work?" he asked, eager to get out of the hospital ward and make sure Amos was gone.

Sigmund chuckled. "Wanna get back at those bastards? I don't blame you, but give yourself some time. The doctors said you'll be better before the end of the month, ready for duty once we move to Brennenbach! Don't worry: we'll keep searching for those sons-of-bitches while you're laid up."

"Thank you, sir."

Sigmund Rahm gave Franz a farewell and a Heil-Hitler, then left him to recover.

DETERMINATION WAS A POWERFUL DRUG, and Franz managed a speedy recovery. He called HQ and asked for a day off after he was released from the hospital to have some time by himself. Edmund Rahm granted this request without hesitation.

"I know Dietrich was your friend," Edmund said as Franz prepared to hang up the phone, and Franz was shocked by the lack of ice in the *Untersturmführer's* tone. Edmund had never sounded so genuine, so sympathetic.

"Yes, sir," Franz said, the lie stinging his tongue. The amalgam voice had returned, little more than a barely-audible hiss now, more Hitler and Herr Keidel than anything else. *Traitor. Murderer. Demon.*

"Take some time," Edmund said. "Then come back and help us avenge him."

"Yes, sir." He felt like he'd swallowed a lemon.

"Heil Hitler."

"Heil Hitler…"

He hung up and ran to his car. The journey to Keidel Farm took three hours, but to Franz it seemed to be an eternity before he pulled up to the crumbling building.

The door was partially open. He almost knocked it down in his haste to enter.

"Amos! Schatzi?!"

No answer. He peeked in the bedroom.

Nothing.

He's gone. Thank God.

The house felt cold, and with Amos gone, he embraced the frostiness completely, letting it enter his heart and form a shield around his soul. Amos was gone and Franz was still alive. Alive and awful in every way. *Traitor. Queer. Jew-lover. Murderer. Demon.*

He inhaled deeply, forcing every warm emotion Amos had made him feel to leave his body, forcing all thoughts of him to vanish. He was gone. Him and all the temptation that went with him. Gone and safe, and now…

Now you need to be a proper SS man again, he thought. *You have to make up for this. For everything you've done. For what you did to Dietrich…*

He gritted his teeth and clenched his fists, glancing in the mirror and inspecting his reflection. Bandaged and pale but ensconced in the mantle of the SS. He needed to become worthy of the uniform again.

Because no matter what, Hitler was right. Franz had been wrong. He had sinned, and now he needed to sin no more. Whatever was left of his soul belonged completely to the Cause now. This mistake would become nothing more than a memory. A pleasant memory. A good memory. Wrong and wonderful all at once.

As he stared at his reflection, something resting on the mattress caught his eye. A familiar tattered rectangle laying on the sloppily-made bedsheets. He shuffled towards it and the ice encasing fractured when he saw what it was: *White Fang.*

Did he forget it? Franz thought, almost hurt by that musing. He picked up the forbidden book and when the heavily creased paper front flew open, he realized there was writing inside, right under the title page.

Every word was like an icepick chipping away at the shield he had summoned around his soul.

Hahnchen,

I realized a little too late that I didn't have any paper to write a farewell letter, and you know I hate ripping pages out of books. Wouldn't want to split anything else up, there's enough of that going on already! It's fine, though. This book is very important to me, and I want you to have it. Any time you begin to feel bad, I want you to read this book aloud and pretend like I'm there listening.

I don't have nearly enough space to write everything I want to say, so I'll try to keep this brief. I've loved every moment we've spent together, from when we were children, when we were lovers, every moment with you has been happy even when we were afraid. Being apart from you again is going to be painful, but I know it won't be forever. I think we've always been destined to be together. We somehow can't stay apart, even when the world wants to keep us from one another. So please don't give up on us. I'm absolutely sure you'll be wrangling orphans before you know it!

You've done so much for me, Hahnchen. I felt like I was losing myself before we reunited. Really, I think you saved my life that day when you found me in Winkler's barn, in more ways than one. I know you think I'm an optimist, and I try to be, but it was hard before.

The Nazis saw me as less than an animal, and I felt like a burden to Winkler, like an obligation. I was beginning to feel like I wasn't even a person, but then you came, and you looked at me as **me**, *as Amos. That meant everything to me then, and it means everything to me now. In a world full of hate, you gave me love. I'm so grateful for that.*

I feel awful leaving now, not just because I love you, but because I feel like I'm abandoning you. Leaving you with the wolves. I'm worried, but I know deep down that you'll be alright. I meant it when I said I'll love you no matter what. Whatever you've done in the past is the past. From now on, think only of the future. I know that you're a wonderful person, and I know that you'll be all right.

Here, the Black Fox must have interrupted Amos, for his handwriting became sloppier in his haste to finish.

I'll see you again, and I love you.
Your Amos.

Franz stared at Amos' signature for too long. The ice cracked, but he didn't let it break. He forced the ice to reform, fixing the fracture.

Silly Amos. Amos the optimist.

He held the book close for a moment, looking down at the steely-eyed wolf-dog on the spine. The house was cold without Amos to warm it. Without Amos to rush forward and embrace him and kiss him.

He exhaled and trudged back into the living room. A few dusty logs provided kindling for the fireplace. The warmth from the crackling fire he created didn't make the ice crack again, but glancing at Amos' message did. He stared at the words and imagined Amos hastily scrawling them, smiling that damned smile of his as he stupidly continued to believe that Franz was something he simply wasn't.

Franz shut the book, spared one glance at the tamed wolf-dog, and did as he had so many times in the past. He tossed the banned book into the flames. The inferno consumed the wolf-dog's visage and Amos' hopelessly optimistic words.

He doused the fire once the book was ashes and left the house feeling whole and cold.

EPILOGUE

Brennenbach, December 31st, 1943

"Hey, Keidel! Wanna beer?"

Sergeant Franz Keidel, who had been standing guard outside one warehouse at the Brennenbach concentration camp, looked up at his comrade. Mueller, whose first name he was still studiously keeping himself from learning, was holding two beers and a bottle opener.

"I'm good," Franz said. "Don't really drink."

"Bah! Your loss! More for me! It's New Year's, come on, lighten up a bit!"

Mueller opened a bottle. The smell was foul and bitter, more odious to Franz than the awful scents coming from the distant *Stehbunker*.

"Thanks, but my family and alcohol don't get along, and besides…" Franz let a small smirk form on his lips. "I wouldn't want to turn into Roschmann."

Mueller let out a loud groan and plopped down on a box full of bullets freshly prepared by the slave laborers of

KZ-Brennenbach. Franz glanced away from his tipsy comrade, watching the Jewish slaves skitter to and fro, urged on by the whips and screams of the SS men on duty. The SS officers were particularly cranky tonight, partially because they hadn't been given the night off to celebrate New Year's in town, and partially because of the Rahm brothers. The Jews paid the price for the Nazis' foul mood.

Franz didn't spare them a thought. He had been a perfect SS man ever since that last day at his family farmhouse. The move to Brennenbach had made it all so much easier: these Jews, shaved and branded with numbers, rendered utterly inhuman, were easy to disregard completely. No curly dark locks reminded him of Am...of *him*.

The Jews of the camp were nameless save for one: the son of the Brennenbach Rabbi. Watching the child had sometimes been hard, seeing his frightened eyes and imagining how much Am...how much *he* would have loved to adopt a helpless little boy like him. But Franz reminded himself that the Rabbi's son wasn't a little boy. No, he was merely a little Jew. And that made it all easier. Even when...

"Hey! Keidel, I feel like I'm talkin' to air here!"

"Huh? Oh, sorry, I was thinking," Franz muttered, shaking his head and nodding at Mueller, who grunted and downed almost half his beer bottle.

"Too much thinking going on 'round here! Kommandant's been *thinking* all fuckin' day, didn't even wanna go to the party! Sent his little brother, and I'm just pissed I can't be in town to witness that shitshow!"

"Especially after this morning," mumbled Franz. "The Kommandant, is he all right? He's had it rough since...well, for a while now, really."

"I'm not checkin' on him! I swear, this town *is* cursed!

Sigmund was nice before, but ever since he became Kommandant...he's making me wish I'd stayed a jeweler."

"That's stress, not a curse," Franz sighed. "With everything that's happened, can you blame him for being upset?"

"Ugh, you...you're just like the Kommandant, you don't believe in anything."

"I believe in the Führer," Franz muttered, gritting his teeth. The amalgam voice had gone quiet long ago, since *he* had left and Franz had paid his indulgences through service to the Cause.

Still, sometimes when he let his thoughts wander, when he remembered what he'd done and how much he didn't regret it, he would hear it. Barely a whisper, more of a choke, threatening to return if he dared to question his Führer again.

"Brown-nose!" cackled Mueller, chucking a bottle cap at Franz. The cap struck Franz's chest and fell to the blood-soaked dirt.

"You sure you don't wanna drink?" Mueller said. "C'mon, it's New Year's soon! Toast with me even if you don't drink!"

Guilt tore at Franz's ice-encased soul. He had tried his best to keep to himself since Am...since *he* had gone away. He hated the idea of becoming friends with any of his comrades after what he had done to Hans Dietrich.

Still, one toast would do no harm. Mueller looked pretty plastered anyway. Not as plastered as Roschmann was wont to get, but plastered enough that he probably wouldn't remember any hint of friendship come morning.

"Sure," Franz said, accepting the almost-empty bottle. Mueller hooted happily.

"All right, what shall we toast to?" Mueller asked.

"The Führer?"

"Ha! Sure, but let's also toast to something...something for us!"

"Hm...to...a better year?" Franz suggested. In the distance, he could hear the citizens of Brennenbach beginning to cheer.

"A better year!" Mueller laughed, clinking his beer bottle against Franz's, taking a celebratory sip as the sound of Germans counting down the seconds grew louder.

"Eleven, ten, nine, eight..."

They never got to one.

Fire rained from the clouds, from Allied aircraft that had taken advantage of the strange mist that had fallen upon Brennenbach that night. The deafening cries of the Germans' celebrations had masked the roar of the bombers' engines. The festive lights offered a clear target.

It was a better death than the Nazis deserved and worse than anything the Jewish prisoners stranded with their tormenters had earned. Bombs set Brennenbach ablaze. The camp was consumed in fire. The lucky ones were killed by the initial explosion or the shrapnel that flew through the air.

Franz was one such fortunate. He only felt his skin melting and his flesh smolder for but a moment before a pain like nothing he had ever felt ripped through him as his soul was torn from its mortal shell.

Pain. Pain. Pain.

Then, nothing for a moment. Coldness, a strangely stifling sensation like he had been stuffed in a bag.

And then, just as he was beginning to think that this was the eternal oblivion that awaited all souls after death, he opened his eyes.

"Congratulations, you're dead."

And found himself standing in a white room.

More specifically, he stood before a cloaked woman wearing a strange mask: a curved mirror that covered her entire face and made it so that when he looked at her, he gazed upon his own distorted reflection. The woman sat at a small desk, looking down at a slip of paper despite the fact that her mask didn't seem to have any holes for her eyes.

Before Franz could even begin to recover from his ordeal, the woman pulled a small party horn seemingly out of thin air and held it up to her masked face, somehow blowing on it despite the mask covering her lips. The accompanying "toot!" echoed through the strange room.

"I...what...agh!" Franz yelped as the strange woman tossed confetti at his face. He leapt back and reached for his gun by instinct, but immediately he realized that while he was still adorned in the SS uniform he had been wearing before the bombing, he was no longer armed.

"You have lived a long and fruitful life of..." The woman leaned closer to the paper clutched in her grey-gloved hand. "Twenty-three years. Your emotional state is very important to us, Soul Number 122-1084369458723408, aka Franz Keidel, child of Johannes Keidel and Sofia Schwartz-Keidel. Therefore, we encourage you to take this time to adjust to your current circumstances."

She paused for an entire two seconds.

He spared a brief glance about the room. There wasn't much to see. The desk was stacked high with papers that he couldn't read from where he was standing. The walls and floor were white, seemingly made out of some sort of stone though it had an odd glow to it. There was a rather dinky chair sitting in one corner with a sign that said "Waiting Room" right next to it.

Besides that, there was a door with a plaque on it that merely boasted two golden triangles, one pointing up and the other pointing down. Two small figures stood on either side of the triangle door. While the woman at the desk wore gray, the two tiny "guards" wore hooded red cloaks and mirror masks concealing their faces. They stood with soldierly discipline, each grasping a wooden sword, making them appear even more like children.

The desk-woman spoke again: "In a moment, you will be examined to ensure that your soul is fit to stand trial. After that, you will be judged before your Creator. Please refrain from asking any questions about the nature of the universe during your trial. Please do not interrupt your counsel or the prosecutor during the trial. Please do not scream or beg for mercy during the trial. Please be advised that this trial is not the work of any alternative deity and/or demonic creature, and please be advised that all judgements are final and not subject to appeal."

Franz's eyes flitted up to a banner that hung above the woman's head. A simple logo of an eye with a white flame for a pupil greeted him. The pain of death ebbed away, and he felt an awful wave of terror wash over him.

A trial was unnecessary. Franz knew exactly where he was going. The only question was why he'd be going there.

"I'm in trouble…" he whispered softly. "Aren't I?"

The woman finally looked up from her paper, and although he couldn't see where her gaze was falling as the reflective mask only offered him a view of his own dismayed expression, he could feel the swastika on his arm burn. She let out a heavy sigh.

"Kid," the angel said, her bored tone breaking into something between pity and glee. "You have *no* idea."

Franz's story will be continued in future books by Elyse Hoffman.

Amos' story will continue in ***The Vengeance of Samuel Val.***

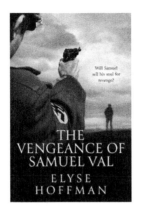

If you enjoyed this story, you'll also enjoy Elyse Hoffman's *Where David Threw Stones,* available for purchase on Amazon.

A NOTE TO MY READERS...

Thank you for reading *Fracture: A Holocaust Story*!

If you enjoyed my novel, please tell your friends! I'd love hear your thoughts on *Fracture: A Holocaust Story*, and reviews help authors a great deal, so I'd be very grateful if you would post a short review on Amazon and/or Goodreads.

If you would like to read more stories like this one and get notifications about free books and short stories, follow Elyse Hoffman on Twitter @Project613Books, on Facebook, and sign up for updates and freebies at elysehoffman.com! You can also follow Elyse Hoffman on BookBub!

AN EXCERPT FROM: WHERE DAVID THREW STONES

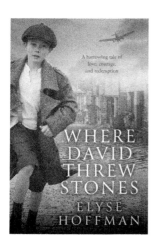

IT HAD BEEN FIVE AND a half weeks since David Saidel killed his parents, and the ten-year-old still despised the mere idea of getting in a car. In Munich there was a dearth of public transportation and his phobia had been catered to: court appointments, police interviews, hospital visits, all easy enough to reach by bus, subway, or train.

But his grandfather's house was far away from the big city and its many travel options. His reclusive Grandpa Ernst resided in a village by the name of Brennenbach, a village so small David hadn't been able to find it on a map. There was no train that stopped in Brennenbach, no bus or subway. The only way to get there was to drive.

"Sorry about this, Davie," Gerta the social worker said, peering into the rearview mirror and offering the boy a smile. If Gerta had a last name, she hadn't been keen to share it with the boy, insisting to the point of aggression that he call her Gerta.

Tempestuously friendly, that was Gerta. Her kindness was as intense as any other human's wrath. She was a plump old lady with a history of fostering Jewish children —in secret during Hitler's reign and proudly after his demise. She had offered to foster David when the boy had ignorantly declared that he had no family left, but David's grandfather had called, declaring himself to be David's new guardian. Some paperwork from David's mother had confirmed that, despite David's assumptions, his grandfather had not perished in the Holocaust.

"Your Opa lives a little out of the way—well, a *lot* out of the way. The railroad to Brennenbach got bombed and was never reconnected. Sorry, Davie, I know you and cars are still...well, on bad terms..."

"It's okay, Gerta," David said. It wasn't, but it was better than staying close to home and receiving one more *I'm-sorry-for-your-loss*. He would move to the most isolated part of West Germany if it meant never having to receive another condolence.

David laid down across the backseat and curled into a fetal position, trying to fall asleep. He opened one eye and brushed some of his flame-colored hair out of his face. They had come to a stop, and Gerta was craning her neck to look back at him. She smiled, and though manners mandated he smile in return, he couldn't. He hadn't smiled since the accident, and he was determined to never smile again.

"Have you ever been to Brennenbach, David?" Gerta asked.

"No, ma'am," he answered. His father, Isak Saidel, had been a writer by trade, a passionate storyteller, especially where it concerned the sad story of his family. He had talked and typed about his mother, his father, his siblings, all of whom had been butchered by Hitler. David's mother, however, had never spoken about her parents or any of her wartime experiences. David, who was not a nosy boy by nature, had never even considered asking.

"Well...your mother didn't cut contact. He knew where you were...he knew a lot about you, actually. He mentioned you and your father playing Skee-Ball, and he said there's an arcade in Brennenbach. So...he won't be a *total* stranger."

David turned his back on the social worker.

"It's fine," he said, squeezing his eyes shut. He knew she wouldn't let it go, she wouldn't just accept those two words. Although he was grateful for her kindness, he felt his chest burn with ire when she inevitably kept at it.

"I know it's not fine, David," she said. "It's perfectly fine for you to *not* be fine, and I want you to know that if something goes wrong, I will be a phone call away. If something goes wrong, you *have* to tell me...David, you *will* tell me, yes?"

"Yes, ma'am..." he said, pressing his face against the car seat's backrest, which smelled of pine. She must have had the car cleaned just for him. He wanted to vomit.

"Please don't think that you're a bother. I know you're thinking that...I know you haven't been thinking good thoughts, David, but you must consider your own health and happiness. Your mama and papa would have wanted you to be happy..."

David had not eaten breakfast or lunch that day, and he was grateful for that. If his stomach had been digesting anything right then, he would have hacked it into Gerta's perfectly perfumed car. She kept going on and on, and he

159

wanted to cover his ears and scream for her to *be quiet, just shut up, please shut up,* but he kept his jaw clenched. He wanted to scream. *They would have wanted to be alive, too…*

Where David Threw Stones is available on Amazon now!

ABOUT THE AUTHOR

Elyse Hoffman is an award-winning author who strives to tell historical tales with new twists. She loves to meld WWII and Jewish history with fantasy, folklore, and the paranormal. She has written eight works of Holocaust historical fiction: the five books of The Barracks of the Holocaust, The Book of Uriel, Where David Threw Stones and Fracture. If you love history and want to read some completely unique stories, follow Elyse at elysehoffman.com.

ALSO BY ELYSE HOFFMAN

The Book of Uriel

Where David Threw Stones

Fracture

The Barracks Novella Series

Barracks One

Barracks Two

Barracks Three

Barracks Four

Barracks Five

Printed in Great Britain
by Amazon

52462530R00098